COMPUTER
CONFUSION

"Saved by the Bell" titles include:

Mark-Paul Gosselaar: Ultimate Gold
Mario Lopez: High-Voltage Star
Behind the Scenes at "Saved by the Bell"
Beauty and Fitness with "Saved by the Bell"
Dustin Diamond: Teen Star
The "Saved by the Bell" Date Book

Hot fiction titles:

COMPUTER CONFUSION

by Beth Cruise

Collier Books
Macmillan Publishing Company
New York
Maxwell Macmillan Canada
Toronto
Maxwell Macmillan International
New York   Oxford   Singapore   Sydney

Collier Books
Macmillan Publishing Company
866 Third Avenue
New York, NY 10022
Maxwell Macmillan Canada, Inc.
1200 Eglinton Avenue East
Suite 200
Don Mills, Ontario M3C 3N1
Macmillan Publishing Company is part of the Maxwell Communication
Group of Companies.
First Collier Books edition 1994
Printed in the United States of America
10 9 8 7 6 5 4 3 2 1

Library of Congress Cataloging-in-Publication Data

Cruise, Beth.
Computer confusion / by Beth Cruise.—1st Collier
Books ed.
p.   cm.
"Saved by the bell"—Cover.
Summary: During spring break, Jessie is busy trying to help Slater pass
history while Zack and Screech go to work at Mr. Morris's new computer
software company and try to keep it from being ruined.
ISBN 0-02-042784-0
[1. High schools—Fiction. 2. Schools—Fiction. 3. Computers—
Fiction.] I. Title.
PZ7.C88827Co 1994
[Fic]—dc20   93-45805

**To all the
"Saved by the Bell"
whiz kids**

Chapter 1

▼　▲　▼　▲　▼

Lisa Turtle flopped down on the beach blanket and dug her toes into the warm sand. It was a perfect day at Palisades Beach. The blue Pacific sparkled, and the afternoon sun was bright but not too hot.

She grinned at her five friends, who were already sprawled on Jessie Spano's old chenille bedspread. The gang had headed for Palisades Beach as soon as the last bell had rung at Bayside High. It was a start-of-spring-break tradition.

"Fifty-five hours and twenty-two minutes," she said happily. "Give or take a couple of seconds."

"What's that, Lisa?" Zack Morris said, his hazel eyes dancing. "The amount of time it takes you to get ready for a dance?"

"Don't be ridiculous, Zack," Lisa replied scornfully.

"Really, Zack," A. C. Slater said. He nudged his friend, nearly sending Zack over backward. Sometimes muscular Slater didn't realize his own strength. "It takes her much longer than that."

"It's the prep time that gets you," Lisa agreed.

The rest of the gang laughed. They were all best friends, who'd known each other for years. They were used to teasing each other about their individual quirks. Gorgeous Lisa didn't need to primp to be pretty, but she enjoyed the effort too much to ever give it up. To her, clothes and makeup were right up there with Mom and apple pie when it came to being an all-American girl.

Kelly Kapowski flipped her long, dark hair over her shoulder and tilted her face to the sun. "Seriously, Lisa," she said. "What's fifty-four hours?"

"Fifty-*five*," Lisa corrected. "Screech calculated how much more free time I could spend with Jeff since it's spring break."

Suddenly, Samuel "Screech" Powers popped up from where he'd been lying, shielding his pale face from the sun with a bright orange towel.

"The margin for error is only point five," he said. "I had to minus weekends, which she would have had off, anyway, and then time for sleeping and eating. It wasn't very hard," he said modestly. "Now I have to finish catching rays." Screech flopped back down and pulled the towel over his face.

"Screech, where exactly *are* you catching rays?" Lisa said. "You're completely dressed."

It was true. Screech was wearing his purple pants and a yellow T-shirt. He was even wearing a striped vest and his zebra-patterned high-tops.

"Nanny says she loves a guy with a tan, but my skin is very sensitive," Screech said, pushing the towel aside so that he could talk. He was dating Nanny Parker, who worked on the school paper. "I thought I'd start out with my elbows and go on from there."

"Screech, you can't tan your elbows," Kelly said. "I've discovered that on my personal quest for the perfect tan."

"*You* tried to tan your elbows, Kelly?" Jessie Spano asked, shielding her eyes from the sun.

"Just one time," Kelly said in a small voice. "I mean, I'm a cheerleader. I have a reputation to maintain. But even I gave up after about five minutes, Screech."

"Don't bother, Kelly," Zack said. "You can't use logic with Screech. It's a waste of time. You might as well try to teach an elephant to fly."

Screech pushed his towel to the side. One blue eye beamed at Zack. "I don't think elephants are that smart, Zack. Besides, how could they ever fit in the cockpit?"

"Let's get back to Jeff," Lisa said. "The next best thing to being with him is talking about him. I hardly ever get to see him."

Lisa's boyfriend went to Stansbury University. His rich and powerful family had a beautiful ranch in the Palisades hills, so he came home frequently.

"Only every weekend," Jessie teased. But when her hazel eyes rested on Slater, her expression clouded. At least Lisa had the man of her dreams. Jessie had lost hers. Slater had broken up with her weeks before, and her heart still hadn't gotten over it.

"You're really lucky, Lisa," Kelly said, her deep blue eyes rueful. "You have a whole week off. I'll be working extra shifts at the yogurt shop. I'll be lucky if I can squeeze in a couple extra dates with Zack."

"Don't worry, Kelly," Zack said craftily. He slid his arm around her. "I'll do the squeezing."

Kelly laughed and snuggled closer. "You'll be too busy working with your father to see much of me, anyway."

"Whoa," Jessie said. She took off her baseball cap and ran a hand through her mass of long curls. "Did you just say Zack would be *working* during vacation, Kelly? Are you talking about *our* Zack Morris? He's allergic to work."

"But this is for dear old dad," Zack said.

Zack's father had recently started a small software company called Intelpro. He and Zack's mother had sunk all their money into the venture, and if it succeeded, Zack was planning on a little red Corvette for his eighteenth birthday.

"What will you be doing, preppy?" Slater asked.

"Interviewing executive secretaries? Remember to check their typing skills *and* their legs."

Jessie frowned as she put her cap back on and pushed the brim down to shade her face. "That's really sexist, Slater. Men can be secretaries, too, you know."

"Whoops. Raging feminist alert," Slater said, waving his hands. "Everyone to the nearest bomb shelter."

Jessie opened her mouth to snap back a retort, but she ended up pressing her lips together. One of the reasons she and Slater had broken up was because he'd said she argued with him all the time. Jessie was trying to change that. But it was hard when he made so many stupid, sexist comments. She loved the guy, but sometimes his brain was sunk in Neanderthal ooze.

Lisa decided it was time to change the subject. If Jessie and Slater got started, there would be a tornado on Palisades Beach, and she'd just washed her hair.

"Zack, you don't know anything about computers," Lisa said. "What *are* you going to do?"

"There's a zillion details when it comes to starting up a company," Zack said, waving his hand loftily. "Executive decisions, product management, long-term goals—"

"He's in charge of making sure everyone has their office supplies," Kelly said, giggling.

The gang laughed. "Pens are very important," Zack protested. "Just ask Mr. Bic." But he couldn't help grinning. "Sure it isn't the biggest job at the company. But it's the tiny details that are driving my dad crazy. I just want to help out. Besides, Screech is going to come with me and help out, too."

"Excuse me?" Lisa said. "You're going to allow Screech through the doors of a brand-new company?"

"Watch out, Intelpro," Slater snickered. "Your days are numbered."

Screech spoke up from underneath the towel. "Hey, if you're going to insult me, do it to my face."

"Okay," Slater said agreeably. "You're a jinx."

Screech's wiry curls bobbed crazily as he shot up to a sitting position. "I'm pink?" He twisted his arm into an impossible position and tried to examine his elbow. "I'd better put on sunscreen."

"Not pink, Screech, *jinx*," Jessie said, laughing. "Slater is just pointing out that you have a tendency to, ah, complicate things sometimes."

"Try *destroy*," Slater said.

"I don't know what you're talking about," Screech said huffily.

"How about the time Lisa was sick, so you said you'd bake cookies for the children's ward at the hospital?" Slater reminded him. "You decided to bake them in a huge pile of dough in a turkey pan and then cut them up later?"

"Only you forgot about them, and they came out like a stone mountain," Kelly said.

"So you tried to slice them with my dad's power saw," Lisa added.

"And cut off the end of the Turtles' dining room table," Jessie finished.

"Well, if you're going to *nitpick*," Screech said.

"Or how about the time you said you'd help Nanny clean her pool?" Slater said. "You dumped a whole box of laundry detergent in it."

"And it happened to be the day Mr. Parker had invited his boss's family over for a swim," Jessie said.

"They all got really clean," Screech pointed out. "I still don't see—"

"Wait, guys," Kelly said. "How about the time Screech gave the entire swimming team pneumonia?"

"Hey, just a second," Screech said indignantly. "That was Zack's idea. He wanted to have a skating party."

"But I didn't think you'd try to freeze the school swimming pool, Screech," Zack said. "Look, guys, I agree that Screech's enthusiasm sometimes takes a wacky turn. But we're talking computers here. He's an expert."

"I've come up with a virus protection program that can be built right into Mr. Morris's software system," Screech said. "Zack is going to ask Mr. Morris if I can implement it."

"Are you sure you want to do that, Zack?" Kelly asked doubtfully. "I mean, it's not like I don't have confidence in Screech's computer skills. But if anything goes wrong . . . well, you've just started to get along better with your dad. I'd hate to see anything spoil that."

"Don't worry, Kelly," Zack said. "I have complete confidence in Screech. And, besides, if it doesn't work, he'll just zap it out of the program. Meanwhile, I'll make sure everyone's happy with their stationery. It will be a cinch."

"Well, all I know is, I'd rather be pushing pencils than what *I* have to do this week," Slater said with a groan. "I'm going to be hitting the books all week. I flunked my history midterm, and Mr. Loomis agreed to give me a makeup test. I've got to do well or I won't get my grade up past a *D*."

"Talk about the impossible dream," Lisa murmured. Slater didn't have the best study habits. He was too easily distracted by TV or food or a good set of waves breaking at the beach.

"I'll help you, Slater," Jessie offered casually. "I aced the midterm, and I still have my notes."

"You'd help *me*?" Slater asked doubtfully.

Jessie shrugged. "Sure. My schedule's pretty light."

Kelly and Lisa exchanged glances. Jessie's nonchalance didn't fool them one bit. They knew she was looking at study sessions as a way to see Slater alone. Jessie might be able to hide her true feelings from Slater, but when it came to her girlfriends, she was an open book.

Lisa crossed her eyes at Kelly in an exasperated way, and Kelly stifled a giggle. It wasn't that they didn't want Jessie to be happy. But Jessie and Slater together had always been an explosive combination. They'd definitely have to run for cover if Slater versus Spano was lining up for a rematch!

Chapter 2

▼　▲　▼　▲　▼

Zack and Screech drove to Kelly's house Monday morning. Zack was planning to drop her off at the mall for her Yogurt 4-U shift and then drive to Intelpro. Mr. Morris had leased warehouse office space on the east side of Palisades.

Kelly was waiting on the porch in her peach-colored uniform, and she waved and ran toward them when they pulled up. She stood outside the car door, and Screech smiled at her.

"Hi, Kelly. You look great. You look like my favorite frozen yogurt flavor, peach melba," Screech said.

"Hi, Screech," Kelly said. "Could you, uh, let me in?"

Screech scrunched over in the passenger seat.

Kelly gave him a pointed look, and he scrunched over even farther, hitting Zack in the chin with his elbow.

"Ow!" Zack cried.

Screech peered at his elbow. "You think *you* got hurt? That scraped my sunburn."

"Screech," Zack said patiently, "will you get into the *back*seat, please?"

"Ah," Screech said knowingly. "You want to sit together. I get it. You don't have to hit me on the head." He started to get out of the Mustang and bonked his head on the roof.

"Looks like you can handle that all by yourself," Kelly said, laughing as she slid in beside Zack. She gave him a kiss. "Thanks for driving me to work."

"It's probably the only way I'll get to see you this week," Zack replied, backing out of the driveway. He headed down Kelly's street toward Palisades Boulevard.

"We're all so busy. Is this what grown-up life is like?" Kelly asked with a sigh.

"Let's hope not," Zack replied. "Having a job sure cuts in on your leisure time. I'm planning on being independently wealthy after my dad makes several million dollars."

"Tell me about your dad's new software again," Kelly said as she settled into her seat. "I keep spacing out when you try to explain it. It's called Timesaver, right? What exactly does it do?"

"Everything," Zack said. "It keeps track of family life. Everything from taxes and car payments to kids' inoculations and dental appointments."

"How does it work?" Kelly asked.

"Say you sit down today or on any Monday morning," Zack said. "You press the calendar function key, and the system prints out everything that's coming up for the week. Junior's soccer game, a mortgage payment, a six-month checkup at the dentist."

"It will even keep track of amounts and write checks for you, like for car payments," Screech said.

"It sounds super," Kelly said, impressed.

"The best part about it, and the thing my dad is banking on, is that it's real easy to learn," Zack explained.

"Even you could learn it, Kelly," Screech piped up.

"Gee, thanks, Screech," Kelly said dryly.

"Don't mention it."

Zack grinned. "And it's also going to be cheaper than anything similar on the market."

"It sounds like it can't lose," Kelly said.

"That's what my dad is hoping," Zack said. "Not to mention the red Corvette I'm hoping to get on my birthday."

Within minutes, they were at the mall. Zack squeezed Kelly's hand and said good-bye. "I'll try to drop by after dinner tonight," he promised.

Kelly grinned. "Just give me time to get the coconut flakes out of my hair."

Zack and Screech drove on to Intelpro. When Zack pulled into the parking lot, he was surprised to see his father getting into his car.

"Hey, Dad, what's up?" Zack called through the car window. "Aren't I supposed to be meeting you in your office right now? I'm not even late yet."

Mr. Morris walked over. He leaned down to the car window, a frown on his face. "Hi, Zack. Hi, Screech. Listen, something's come up. I just got a call from a business associate in San Francisco. He says there's a rumor that another software company's coming out with a program similar to Timesaver and they're planning to release it at the software expo next week, just like we are. I have to go up to San Francisco and check it out. This could ruin us."

Zack's worried frown was just like his father's. "Do you think it could be true?"

Mr. Morris shrugged. "Who knows? I hope not. I'm confident that our product can beat out the competition. It's just that the timing couldn't be worse."

"I'm sure you'll still come out ahead, Mr. Morris," Screech said. "Timesaver is mondo cool."

Mr. Morris smiled wryly. "Can I quote you on that for *UserFriendly* magazine, Screech?" Mr. Morris checked his watch. "Listen, I have to run.

I'm catching the ten o'clock shuttle, and I have to drive by the house to pick up my suitcase. I left instructions with Mrs. Smedley, my personal assistant, to show you around. She'll introduce you to Miles Moriarity, the chief software engineer. He's already lining up new products for the company, so be nice to him. He's a genius. I had a heck of a time wooing him away from Quiksystems. He brought over his two favorite hackers, too. The only way they'd come was if I'd give them complete freedom."

"We'll treat them with kid gloves," Zack promised.

"Gee, Zack, I don't know if I can work on the keyboard in *gloves*," Screech said. "Besides, I don't even have any. Maybe a catcher's mitt, but that's—"

"Don't worry, Dad," Zack interrupted, putting his hand over Screech's mouth. "I'll gag him."

Mr. Morris grinned. "Thanks for keeping an eye on things, Zack. I'll call tonight. And I'll be back next Monday morning."

Zack watched Mr. Morris hurry off to his car. "Dad's under a lot of pressure," he said. "If that system really is too similar to Timesaver, we'll be in trouble. I wish there was some way I could help him besides making sure everyone has enough pencils."

"We didn't get a chance to tell him about my virus protection program," Screech said.

"Right," Zack said. He frowned thoughtfully as he pulled into a space.

"We can tell him when he gets back," Screech said. "If the rumor's true, it might cheer him up. Of course, I don't know for *sure* if the program works." Screech opened the car door and got out.

"Right," Zack said absentmindedly to the empty car. He called out through the open car window. "Hey, Screech, what if we don't wait?"

Screech's frizzy curls flattened as he squeezed his head back through the window. "Wait for what?"

"Wait for my dad to get back," Zack said. "What if you input the program while he's gone? It will be a great surprise."

"If it works," Screech said.

"Of course it will work," Zack said. "I believe in you, Screech."

Screech frowned. "Even though I'm a jinx?"

"I have complete confidence in you," Zack said sincerely.

"Gosh, thanks, pal," Screech said. "Uh, Zack? Here, let me get the car door for you. It's hard to open it when your fingers are crossed."

▲   ▼   ▲

Kelly got off her shift at the yogurt shop early, and she hurried home to change before meeting Jessie and Lisa at Bayside High. Even though football season was over, the Bayside High team was playing a scrimmage against Valley High. Tickets had been sold the week before in both schools, and the proceeds were going to help fund a citywide Sports Day next year.

"I can't believe we're at school during spring break," Kelly said as she came up to her friends, who were waiting for her on the front steps of the school. "We must be crazy."

"Or one of us is in love," Lisa said, with a pointed glance at Jessie.

Jessie tossed her long brown curls. "I'm just interested in supporting Bayside High sports," she said offhandedly.

Lisa and Kelly burst out laughing. Slater was the captain of the football team, but even when Jessie had gone to games, she'd taken a book so she wouldn't get bored. Every time Slater had looked up in the stands, she'd had to hide it under her sweatshirt.

"I *am*," Jessie insisted. "I, um, have come to recognize and appreciate the amazing strategy that football requires—"

Lisa and Kelly giggled even harder.

"Besides," Jessie said, "the uniforms are cute."

"Now, that I believe," Lisa gasped.

"Come on, Jessie," Kelly said as they made their way to the playing field. "Admit it. The only reason you wanted to come today was because Slater is playing."

Jessie hesitated. "Well . . . ," she said.

"Come on, girl," Lisa said. "Spill it. You still have it in a major way for that curly-haired caveman."

"Okay," Jessie admitted in a rush. "I do. I tried to just be friends, but I can't. And the reason I can't is that I've finally figured out why Slater broke up with me. I tried to run the relationship. I never gave him credit for being smart or doing the right thing. I was bossy and opinionated, and didn't even try to see his side."

"It's true," Kelly and Lisa admitted.

"Hey," Jessie said. "You don't have to agree with me."

"I'm sorry, Jess. But it *is* true," Lisa said. "To be fair, though, I have to say that sometimes Slater was that way, too."

"I was worse," Jessie said morosely.

"It's true," Lisa and Kelly said together.

"Hey!" Jessie said. "I said you didn't have to *agree* with me." She sighed. "Who am I kidding? You're right. Sure, Slater was pigheaded and stubborn and all that. But he was a soft touch underneath. He did stuff that I promised to never tell you guys, like go to poetry readings and make posters for my Save the Whales march."

"Slater did that?" Lisa said.

"He really was crazy about you," Kelly said, and sighed.

The girls took their seats in the bleachers. "That's why I still have hope," Jessie said.

"But, Jessie, Slater seemed so positive this time," Kelly said hesitantly. "He really thinks it's time for both of you to move on."

"I know," Jessie said. "But things are looking up. You saw what happened yesterday."

"Right," Lisa said.

"Right," Kelly echoed. They looked at each other.

"What happened?" they asked Jessie together.

"He asked me to help him study," Jessie said dreamily.

"Uh, Jessie?" Kelly said. "He didn't ask. You offered."

"He said yes," Jessie said, still dreamy eyed.

"So?" Lisa asked. "He's flunking history, and you got the history medal this year."

"It makes perfect sense," Kelly said.

"What if he wants to get back together, but he's too embarrassed to try?" Jessie pointed out. "You know how macho he is. This is a great way for us to spend oodles of time together."

Lisa and Kelly exchanged glances. Somehow they just didn't buy Jessie's theory, but they didn't want to burst her bubble.

"Don't you think it's *possible*?" Jessie urged, her eyes on the field as the Bayside High players streamed out. She raised her chin to get a better view, trying to see Slater.

"Anything is possible," Lisa said.

"Sure," Kelly said. "You know me. I'm an optimist."

Jessie had her eyes trained on Slater, and she failed to notice the doubt in her friends' voices. "I knew you guys would agree," she said.

▲   ▼   ▲

Jessie waited outside the locker room for Slater to emerge. The other players had come out in twos and threes, but Slater was still inside. It wasn't like him to be so late. Usually he was the first one changed and out the door.

But Jessie didn't mind waiting. The spring breeze lifted her hair and wafted softly against her cheeks. Spring was her favorite season. She loved the blossoms and the fresh feeling in the air. She loved the warm nights at the beach, when Slater would build a fire and they would lie back, tracing constellations in the sky.

She would have it again, Jessie knew. She retied her sweatshirt around her neck. By this time next week, she and Slater would be a couple again!

He burst out of the locker room, his face creased in a grin. He must have known she'd be waiting to congratulate him, even though they had planned to meet at the library for a study date.

"Slater," Jessie called.

He looked over at her, surprised. "Oh, Jess. Hi. I didn't see you."

"You were fantastic," Jessie said. "You must have beaten your own record for completed passes. Too bad it wasn't a real game. I guess it didn't count, huh?"

"Actually, it did," Slater said. "Do you know who I was just talking to? The scout for Great Bear University!"

Jessie frowned. "Great Bear? Isn't that near here?"

"It's only an hour away," Slater said. "And it has one of the best college teams in California. Anyway, the scout told me that he could practically *guarantee* me a football scholarship. He talked to Coach Sonski and looked at my records. Do you know what this means, Jessie?" Slater's dark eyes shone. "A four-year scholarship! Awesome!"

"It is pretty awesome," Jessie said. "But I thought you had your heart set on California University. They have the best broadcasting facilities in the state."

Slater's face darkened. "But they're not offering me a penny to go there."

"Well, not yet," Jessie said. "There's still time."

Slater looked at his watch. "Listen, I'd love to stay and talk, but I have to run home and change. The scout wants to take me out to a late lunch at the Beefsteak Club."

Jessie's smile slowly faded from her face. "But we have a study date."

"Oh, right," Slater said. Obviously, he'd completely forgotten. "We can meet later, can't we? This is more important."

"Sure," Jessie said faintly.

"Great. Come to my house around four," Slater said over his shoulder as he hurried toward the parking lot.

Jessie slumped against the wall. Slater was right. Meeting the scout was more important. But there hadn't been one trace of regret in Slater's tone. It was almost like he was actually looking at the study session as . . . well, a study session. The guy sure had a nerve!

Chapter 3

▼ ▲ ▼ ▲ ▼

"Welcome to Intelpro," Eunice Smedley said when she met Zack and Screech at the front security desk. She was a small, motherly woman with a youthful smile. "I'm so glad to meet you," she said to Screech. "You look just like your father."

"Gosh, thanks," Screech said. "Most people say I take after my great-uncle on my mother's side."

"I think she means me, Screech," Zack said.

"*You* look like my great-uncle on my mother's side?" Screech said, twisting to regard Zack. "You've never even been to Toledo."

"Screech—"

"Well, maybe around the chin," Screech mused, staring at Zack's profile.

In frustration, Zack clapped his hand over

Screech's mouth. "Good morning, Mrs. Smedley. I'm Zack Morris," he said.

"Oh, of course," Mrs. Smedley said. "I should have known. You look just like your father, dear. Welcome to Intelpro."

"Thank you," Zack said.

"Mmmmpphhh," Screech said. Zack dropped his hand. "Delighted to be here," Screech added, straightening the collar of his polka-dot shirt.

"Now, your father left instructions that you could work in his office," Mrs. Smedley said. "I'm in the adjoining office, and I'll be happy to help you, Zack. You'll need a key to the supply room, and I'll show you how to access the supply list on the computer."

"On the computer?" Zack gulped. He wasn't exactly a keyboard whiz like Screech.

"Everything at Intelpro is hooked up to our main computer," Mrs. Smedley said, leading them up a flight of gray-carpeted stairs. "That's how we keep track of expenses. If you want to order a pencil from the supply room or fax an order for a tuna sandwich from the deli across the street, you go through Marion. That's what we call the central server," she explained. She stopped at a locked door. "She's behind here."

Zack pictured a giant waitress lurking behind the door. But Screech was nodding respectfully, so Zack knew the central server must be a big computer.

Mrs. Smedley continued briskly down the hall. "Every engineer has his or her own terminal, which is hooked up to Marion. Now, here we are," she finished with a flourish, ushering them into Mr. Morris's office.

Zack had been inside his father's office before, but it hadn't been decorated yet. Mr. Morris had said that he'd have a very limited budget and would probably pick up some secondhand furniture. Zack stopped, surprised. The office looked like something out of *Office Beautiful*.

"Wow," Zack said, looking around. "It looks great!"

The windows that lined one wall had a view of the green and gold hills on the outskirts of Palisades. The furniture was sleek, polished wood. There was a huge black leather couch, and Mr. Morris had a massive oak desk.

Zack dropped into a huge leather desk chair and twirled around. "If this is decorating on a budget, I'd like to see Dad throw some real money around!"

"I found us some deals," Mrs. Smedley said modestly.

Screech was drawn to Mr. Morris's computer terminal and fax, which were on a separate table beside the desk. He clicked a few keys. "I can't wait to run the Timesaver program," he said.

"Dad said Screech could run through it," Zack told Mrs. Smedley.

"Of course," she said. "Have fun. It's an excellent program. Your father is a programming genius, Zack. And a very nice man, I might add. He hired me when no one else would. It's amazing—people think that just because you're over fifty, you don't have a brain anymore."

"Don't worry about it, Mrs. Smedley," Screech said. "I'm only seventeen, and people don't think I have a brain, either."

"We do occasionally have our doubts," Zack told her.

Mrs. Smedley grinned. "Well, I'll just leave you boys now," she said. "I have some work to do. Zack, just let me know when you want to go to the supply room. I'll show you where it is and give you a key."

She closed the door softly behind her. Zack turned to Screech. "Okay, let's go," he said. "Start instituting the virus protection program."

"Are you sure?" Screech asked doubtfully.

"I'm sure," Zack said. "I want to surprise my father."

Screech clicked a few keys and called up Timesaver, Mr. Morris's software program. He sighed, his fingers resting on the keys. "Zack, I hate to break into your dad's computer system without telling him. Of course, I can erase whatever I do . . . I think."

"Just do it, Screech," Zack said. "I've got to do my office supply thing. I'll be back in a jiffy."

"Mmmmm," Screech said. He was already lost in computer jargon.

Zack slipped out of the office and went to Mrs. Smedley's smaller office next door. For the next twenty minutes, he discovered everything he didn't ever want to know about office supplies. Then he checked every office to make sure that everyone had desk chairs and bookcases. He was surprised that the offices were so cool looking. Mr. Morris had made it sound like everyone would have to work out of packing cases for a few months, until they were able to generate some sales.

It was almost an hour before he could return to Screech. Zack walked into the office and found Screech still hunched over the computer terminal.

"How's it going?" he asked.

Screech jumped up. The chair skidded back and slammed against the desk. "Oh, it's you!" he said.

"What's the matter?" Zack asked. "Why are you so nervous?"

Screech rubbed a finger against the back of the chair. "Who, me? I'm not nervous. Why would I be nervous?" Then he gripped the back of the chair, and it started to shake.

Zack advanced cautiously. "Screech, what is it? You can tell me."

Screech gulped. "Well, I started to run my virus protection program. It was going pretty well."

"And?" Zack prompted.

"And, well, this funny thing happened," Screech said, running a hand through his wiry curls. "I mean, it's never happened before. You might find this so funny you'll even laugh—"

"Screech," Zack demanded. *"What funny thing happened?"*

"Well, instead of protecting the system from a virus," Screech said, "I introduced a virus *into* the system. Isn't that funny, Zack?" Suddenly, Screech rolled the chair forward so that it was between them. "Uh, Zack? You're not laughing. At least you'll get to surprise your dad. Uh, Zack? Ow! That's my sunburn!"

▲   ▼   ▲

Later that afternoon, Jessie gathered up all her history books and notes and drove over to Slater's house. Balancing her notebooks and textbooks, she rang the doorbell with her pinky.

Seconds later, Slater threw open the door. "Jessie!" he cried. Suddenly, he picked her up in his arms and swung her around.

Jessie's notebooks and pencils flew through the air, and she laughed giddily. It felt so good to be in his arms again!

"What is it?" she asked breathlessly.

Slater laughed and set her back down on the ground. Jessie was disappointed when his strong arms let her go immediately.

"I got it!" he crowed. "I got a four-year, full scholarship to Great Bear University!"

"Congratulations!" Jessie enthused. "That's fantastic, Slater!"

"Mr. Cramer told me right after lunch," Slater said. "He shook my hand and said I was the kind of athlete Great Bear was looking for. I'll be getting confirmation in the mail, and he wants me to visit the campus sometime this week."

"Wow, a full scholarship," Jessie said, crouching down to pick up her books. "That's really an honor."

Slater bent down to help her. "I can't wait to tell my parents," he said. "They're both at work. Wait until they hear that I'll be going to school only an hour away! I could even live at home to save money."

Jessie paused, her hand on *Our Glorious Constitution.* She looked at Slater. He was crouched down next her, and their faces were very close. His brown eyes were warm and friendly. He reached for *Our Glorious Constitution,* and his fingers brushed hers. The tingle went all the way down to her toes in her cowboy boots.

Don't blow it, Spano, she warned herself. *Don't spoil the moment.*

"What's the matter, Jessie?" Slater asked softly. "I can read you like a book. Well, better than a book, considering my study habits. What's wrong?"

"Nothing," Jessie said carefully. "But did you tell this guy that you'd accept the scholarship?"

"Of course I did," Slater said. "I'm not crazy." His hand slid off the textbook. "Why shouldn't I have?"

"Well," Jessie said slowly as she picked up another book, "it's just that, well, I thought you had your heart set on California University. It's a much better school. And you said yourself you wanted to live in a dorm to get new experiences. Why should you lock yourself into Great Bear?"

Slater picked up the rest of the books and stood up. "Because CU is much more competitive," he said. "They're picking the best high school students from around the whole *country*, Jess. I could never get a four-year scholarship there. And the course work would be a lot harder. I want to concentrate on sports."

"Can't you do both?" Jessie asked.

Slater shrugged. "Why should I make it harder on myself?"

He walked into the house, and Jessie followed him into the living room. "Mr. Cramer is a great guy," he continued. "He said they really need a quarterback with my abilities. The professors at Great Bear understand the importance of the team. He said that he could see me being a real star at Great Bear." Slater grinned. "Can you see me as a big man on campus?"

Maybe a big head *on campus,* Jessie wanted to say.

"Well, Jess?"

"I'm trying," she said.

"So," Slater said. "Why'd you stop by? Are you on your way to the library?" he asked, indicating her books.

She gazed at him incredulously. "Our study session, Slater. You're flunking history. Remember?"

Slater waved a hand in the air. "Study session? Don't need it. I've got a scholarship to Great Bear, remember?"

Dread snaked up Jessie's spine. "What are you talking about, Slater?" she asked.

Slater sank down on the couch and folded his arms. "I've already gotten into college. Why should I study? I'm just going to cruise my way through the rest of high school!"

Chapter 4

▼　▲　▼　▲　▼

"Screech, it's been nearly an hour," Zack said nervously. "What's taking so long?"

"I'm not sure," Screech said, staring at the screen while he clicked the keys.

"It's not because I said I wouldn't kill you until *after* you got the virus out of the system, is it?" Zack asked. "Because it was just a joke."

"I know," Screech said absentmindedly.

"I'm not going to kill you. I'm going to maim you," Zack muttered underneath his breath. He couldn't believe he had trusted Screech. The gang was right: The guy was a jinx. And as soon as he fixed the system, Zack would let him have it.

"It's weird," Screech said. "I can't figure this out. For a user-friendly system, I'm getting the cold shoulder. I even went into plokta mode a couple of times—"

"Plokta mode?" Zack asked desperately. "Is that some sort of high-tech rescue plan?"

"Actually, it stands for 'press lots of keys to abort,'" Screech said, still staring at the screen. "Basically, you just press a bunch of keys and hope something interesting happens."

"I'm glad to see you're approaching this scientifically," Zack said sarcastically.

"It's the only way," Screech agreed. "Now, if only I could figure out why—"

Suddenly, Mr. Morris's office door banged open. Two guys in plaid flannel shirts walked in, arguing so furiously that they didn't even notice Zack and Screech.

"Hal, I told you to stop reading my E-mail," the shorter guy said. He wasn't exactly dressed for success, Zack noted. His flannel shirt had a tear at the elbow, and his baggy corduroy slacks had probably been either gray or green a long time ago.

"It was an accident, Cruncher," a tall, rangy guy with thick, black-rimmed glasses said. "I keep telling you. And maybe if you didn't use the network as a dating service, you wouldn't be so sensitive—"

"I'm not using it as a dating service, dweeb-meister! Miranda was just surfing the system, looking for someone who liked Jerry Lewis movies," the shorter guy complained. "You know I'm nuts for Jerry."

"That might be your problem, nerd-o-matic," the tall guy named Hal said. "The Three Stooges are the way to go. Jerry is bogus."

"Dream on, techno-kook," Cruncher said. "The French think Jerry's a genius. Who are you to argue with the country that invented fries?"

"Next time, use snail mail, you byte-size nitwit-naut," Hal said calmly. "Romance can't handle advanced throughput."

Zack couldn't believe it. Were these guys talking a different language? He'd seen plenty of geeks at Bayside High. But these guys were *genius* geeks.

"What are they talking about?" he whispered to Screech.

"E-mail is electronic mail," Screech murmured. "If you're connected to a computer network, people send messages right to your computer. It's a neat way to meet people. Throughput is how fast information can be propelled through a network. Snail mail means regular mail. And Jerry Lewis is a comedian."

Zack looked back at the two guys. Whoever they were, he had to get them out of his father's office before they started to wonder what Screech was doing at the computer.

Zack moved so he was standing in front of Screech. "Can I help you guys?"

The two looked up, startled. "Who are you?" Cruncher, the short Jerry Lewis fan, bawled belligerently.

"I'm Zack Morris," Zack said.

"Oh, you're the son," Hal said, nodding. "Mr. Morris told us his son would be here." He nudged Cruncher. "Remember, Monsieur Nutty Professeur?"

"Of course I do, weirdomobile," Cruncher said. "Didn't mean to barge in. Mr. Morris said his door was always open."

"It was closed, though," Hal said. "I nearly gave myself a black eye. Bumped into it. Ouch City. What's that guy doing at the computer?"

Quickly, Zack moved toward the two guys. "I'm really glad to meet you two," he said, smoothly ushering them to the door. "I've heard a lot about you. What are your names again?"

"I'm Chris Ciccolini, but you can call me Cruncher," the short one growled. "This is Hal Torrance."

"No nickname," Hal said. "But I was named after the computer in *2001*. Not the year. The movie."

"Right," Zack said, easing them toward the doorway. "Do you guys want some office supplies?" Zack asked. "Paper? Pencils? Index cards?"

"I need more fax paper," Hal said.

"I like those multicolored paper clips," Chris said.

"Great," Zack said. "Why don't I walk you back to your offices and we'll make a list?"

Zack quickly hurried Hal and Chris out of the office. They turned out to be complete office-supply hounds, and by the time he'd gotten them colored index cards and markers and bulletin boards and Rolodex card files, another hour had passed. He ran back to the office, but this time, Screech was pacing and pulling at his already messy hair.

He looked up at Zack wildly. "I'm stuck. I can't think. What's the answer?"

"Pepperoni pizza," Zack said. "You need fuel. It's past lunchtime."

He faxed in an order to the pizza parlor around the corner, and it arrived in ten minutes. Screech inhaled two slices in record time and then ran back to the computer.

Zack tried to concentrate on his own work as Screech clicked away at the keyboard. Mrs. Smedley stuck her head in at four o'clock.

"How is it going, boys? Can I help?"

Zack jumped up. "No, no, we're fine, Mrs. Smedley. Would you care for a slice of pizza?"

"Well, no, I've eaten," Mrs. Smedley said. "But I will take a slice down to Bernice Mooney. Her department has been working around the clock, poor dear. She can heat it up in the microwave."

Zack shoved the pizza box at her. "Give this to Bernice with my compliments, Mrs. Smedley."

She peered over his shoulder. "What is your friend, uh, Scrimp, doing?"

"Screech," Zack said, easing Mrs. Smedley toward the door. "He's doing his homework. Bye, now."

Zack closed the door behind her and continued pacing. He counted his steps from the desk to the door and had reached three thousand and started all over again when Screech sighed and turned around.

"I figured it out," he said, rubbing his eyes.

"Great! All fixed, then," Zack said, relieved.

"Sorry, Zack," Screech said. "But it's not all fixed. We've got a big problem here."

"How big?" Zack said nervously. "Rhode Island or Texas?"

"Try all fifty states and throw in Canada," Screech said.

Zack slumped down on the desk. "Tell me quick," he groaned. "Get it over with."

"The reason I couldn't get my virus out of the program was because there was *another* virus in it already," Screech said. "My program kept beeping that my system was invaded, even though I'd already located my virus and eliminated it. That meant that there was already at least one bug in the system."

"Already? You mean someone put one there?"

Screech nodded. "It's hidden really well. But once I found it, I started looking for others. They're all incredibly tiny and incredibly hard to locate. I wouldn't have found them if I wasn't trying to get rid of mine. The product integrity department here probably missed them. But, Zack, they can completely sabotage parts of the software program."

"How?" Zack said, coming up behind Screech at the terminal.

"Watch," Screech said. "Your father has sample family systems programmed into his computer. I'll run a simple Timesaver function. Say I want to pay a tax bill. I type out FEB, for February, and TAX, for taxes, and INC, for income. Then I press the function key. Now watch."

A message started blinking at the bottom of the screen:

DELETING FILES

"What is it doing?" Zack asked.

"It's deleting my entire address book," Screech said calmly. "Just because I typed in a certain combination of words. There's a bunch of those bugs throughout the system. I already wiped out a section of tax records by asking about an April dental bill."

Zack hung on to the back of Screech's chair. His legs suddenly felt wobbly. "What are you telling me, Screech?"

Screech's face reflected blurrily from the screen in front of him. "I'm saying that there's an industrial spy loose in your father's company," he said. "And if we don't catch him, he'll destroy everything!"

▲   ▼   ▲

Jessie tossed and turned all Monday night, worrying about Slater. Finally, she fell into a heavy sleep and dreamed that the gang was graduating, but that Slater was sitting way in the back of the auditorium. Then Mr. Belding threw a custard pie into his face, and the whole school laughed.

She woke up with a start. She couldn't let Slater be humiliated that way! Before she could change her mind, she flopped over in bed and dialed his number.

He sounded surprised to hear from her, especially since it was seven in the morning, but Jessie didn't care. "Slater, I've been thinking," she said.

"Uh-oh," he said teasingly. "That usually means big trouble for me."

"I just can't stand it if you flunk history," Jessie said. "First of all, I told Mr. Loomis that I was going to tutor you. You'll make *me* look bad."

"Mr. Loomis thinks you're the best thing since the Bill of Rights," Slater said. "I doubt he'd hold it against you. He knows what kind of a hard head I have."

Jessie twisted the phone cord around her finger. "Well, maybe. But I'd feel bad. And a failing grade looks bad on your transcript, no matter where you go to school. I just wish you'd agree to study a little bit. You know how Coach Sonski is always saying that an athlete should be a scholar, too."

Slater snickered. "Coach Sonski's favorite reading material is *Archie* comics," he said. "Try again."

Jessie sighed. Slater could be so stubborn! "How about agreeing to study for *me*?" she asked meekly. "I mean, we're still friends, aren't we?"

Slater broke into a loud guffaw. "Now I know you're off the wall."

Jessie felt stung. Obviously, the thought that he might want to do something for her was absolutely hysterical. She laughed weakly so that he wouldn't think she'd been serious.

"How about your parents?" she persisted. "Your mom will freak if you get an *F.* What will she talk about at the next family party?"

Slater hesitated. It was true. His mother loved to tell all her sisters how great he was doing at school. He hated to disappoint her.

"Okay, Jess," he said slowly. "I'll tell you what. I *will* study for the makeup test."

Jessie shot up to a sitting position. "Fabulous! I think it's definitely the right decision, Slater. Why don't we meet this afternoon? We can start with the Constitutional Convention—"

"Whoa, hold on," Slater said. "I've got one condition. I only study enough to get a *C*-plus. That way, I'll raise my final grade to a *D* and won't flunk the class."

"A *D*?" Jessie practically shouted. "You'll be happy with a *D*?"

"Why not?" Slater said. "What difference does

my grade make as long as I don't fail? Why waste the energy trying for an *A* or a *B*?"

"B-because," Jessie sputtered.

"I've got a clear shot from now on, Jessie. My path is paved with gold. What do I need to know about the Constitution for if I'm a football star? I'll be too busy going to parties and dodging awesome babes hungry for my bod."

"Oh, please," Jessie groaned.

"Hey, don't beg me," Slater said. "You had your opportunity and you blew it, babe. Give the other girls a chance. Today I'm going to catch some rays. If I'm going to visit Great Bear this week, I need to be tan. First impressions are super important. I'll call you."

Jessie stared at the receiver as a dial tone buzzed at her. *Who did I just talk to?* she wondered. Sure, Slater had always had a healthy ego. He had always pretended that he was Bayside High's answer to Arnold Schwarzenegger. But behind all that swagger was only slush. He was the most level-headed guy in the world.

But someone was pumping his head full of talk about how great he was, and it seemed he was having a hard time not believing it. Because this time, Slater had sounded like he *meant* everything he was saying.

Jessie sighed. *Watch out, Palisades Beach. There's an ego out of control heading your way!*

Chapter 5

▼ ▲ ▼ ▲ ▼

"You've got to come through for me, Screech," Zack said Tuesday morning as they pulled into the Intelpro parking lot. "You've got to find the spy today. I'm a wreck. I even forgot to try to get Kelly alone last night. I talked to her mother for an hour in the kitchen! I'm telling you, man, my brain is fried."

"Now you know what it's like to be me," Screech said.

"Please," Zack groaned. "I'm already having nightmares."

"I've got a couple of ideas," Screech said as they hurried toward the building. "First, I've got to fig-ure out a way to find out what time the spy first crashed the system. I can check that against whoever was logged into the computer. Marion logs everybody's computer time on her own clock."

"Whatever you say, Screech," Zack said. "Just find the—" He stopped abruptly and motioned Screech to be quiet. A very tall, sandy-haired man with a long, narrow face was approaching them.

"You must be Zack and Screech," the man said. He pushed up his tortoiseshell glasses and stuck out his hand. "I'm Miles Moriarity, the chief engineer here. Your dad told me to watch out for you guys," he said to Zack.

The guy's long nose twitched nervously. He didn't look like a spy. He looked like a rabbit. But why was he so nervous?

Zack shook his hand and felt something crunch.

"Oops," Miles Moriarity said. He opened his hand and showed Zack and Screech a palmful of crushed peanut shells. "I forgot I was holding my breakfast. Let me know if I can help you guys at all," he said absentmindedly. He ambled away, trailing peanut shells.

What a weirdo, Zack thought. *And maybe even a suspect.*

"Great guy," Screech said admiringly. "We know *he* can't be the spy. He's too nice and normal."

Zack sighed. Having Screech as a detective partner was like working with E.T.

"I'm going to need massive computer time," Screech told Zack as they climbed the stairs to Mr.

Morris's office. "You're going to have to run interference again. Hey, maybe we should call Slater. He's a football player."

"I think we need someone else to run this play," Zack said thoughtfully.

"Who?" Screech asked. "Buster Henderson?"

"Eunice Smedley," Zack answered.

"Wow," Screech said. "I didn't even know she played football."

They hurried down the hall. Zack knocked on Mrs. Smedley's office. She looked up, startled, as they burst in.

"Is anything wrong?"

"Brace yourself, Mrs. Smedley," Zack said. "But we think there's an industrial spy trying to sabotage Timesaver."

Mrs. Smedley put a hand to her heart. "Oh, my. Are you sure?"

Screech nodded solemnly. "He's planting bugs in the system."

Mrs. Smedley frowned. "Now, boys, I know you want to help. But I don't know about this. How could someone break into our system? You need passwords."

"It could be someone *in* the company," Zack pointed out.

"Oh, dear," Mrs. Smedley breathed. "I don't see how that's possible. Everyone is so nice."

Zack put a hand on her shoulder. "Mrs.

Smedley, not everyone is as nice as you are. Now, will you help us?"

Mrs. Smedley sank into her chair. "Of course. What can I do?"

"We have to think of a cover story for why Screech will be working at the computer all day," Zack said. "We can't tip off the spy."

Mrs. Smedley frowned. Then she clapped her hands. "I've got it. I'll say that we're testing to make sure that the Timesaver program can be used by even the most unsophisticated person of, uh, extremely limited skills." She beamed at Screech. "No offense."

"None taken," Screech said brightly. "What does she mean, Zack?" he whispered.

"She means you have to pretend you're a space cadet, Screech," Zack said.

Screech straightened his shoulders. "It'll be a challenge," he said. "But I'll do my best."

▲   ▼   ▲

Wednesday morning, Jessie drummed her fingers on the table.

"Shhhh," the librarian said.

Jessie stopped and looked at her watch. Where was Slater? He'd promised to meet her at the Palisades Town Library at ten sharp. It was almost ten-thirty!

Something was happening to Slater, Jessie

thought gloomily. Yesterday, he'd put off their session so that he could catch rays and get a haircut. Then when they'd rescheduled for this morning, he'd grumbled about the time, because it would cut into his workout—

Jessie sprang to her feet. That muscle-bound bum was probably still at the gym! Leaving her books on the table, Jessie dashed for the door, bumping into a desk on the way. The librarian's *shhhhhhh* followed her out.

The gym where Slater worked out was only a five-minute drive away. Jessie screeched into the parking lot and jumped out of her car. She ran into the gym and checked out the grunters and groaners who were torturing themselves in order to gain just a microinch more of muscle mass.

Finally, she spotted a curly head adjusting a machine to handle extra weight. Jessie strode over and tapped Slater on a sweaty, muscular shoulder.

He turned. "Jessie! Come to work out?"

"I came to get you," Jessie said tersely. "We had a date, remember?"

Several of the guys around Slater snickered.

"Bad news, hotshot," one of them said.

"Looks like you messed up, lover boy," another one said.

Slater blushed. "It wasn't a *date*," he said out loud. "It was an *appointment*."

One of the muscle-bound guys looked at Jessie's

curls and her long, long legs in faded jeans. "What, are you nuts?" he said. He winked at Jessie. "If this ox doesn't come through, I'm available."

Jessie grinned and tossed her curls. "But are you interested in everything you ever wanted to know about the Bill of Rights but were afraid to ask?" she asked flirtatiously.

"Now I am," he shot back. "It's my very favorite subject."

"I *love* the Bill of Rights," another guy called. "What are they, anyway?"

Slater flushed in annoyance and grabbed Jessie's elbow. "Let's get out of here, momma," he growled. "You're going to start a riot."

Jessie giggled as he swept her out of the gym. "I'm glad to see you're so enthusiastic about studying now," she said.

"Hey, give me a break," Slater said. "My body is a temple, babe."

Jessie stopped in her tracks. "Slater, we did have an appointment," she said. "I've been waiting at the library for thirty minutes."

Slater sighed. "I'm sorry, Jess. Listen, just let me hit the shower. I'll meet you at the library in fifteen minutes. I promise."

"Just don't stop to bench-press anything on the way," Jessie said, striding out the door.

Jessie was ready to blast Slater for being one second late, but he showed up at the library in fifteen minutes with damp curls and a guilty grin.

"I only have an hour," he whispered to her.

"What?" Jessie said. "We can't get anything done in an hour."

He shrugged. "I can't help it. I have an appointment."

"An appointment or a *date*?" Jessie asked sarcastically. She knew she shouldn't press Slater, but she couldn't help it. A girl could only keep her mouth shut so long.

"An appointment," Slater said, opening a textbook. "With a freshman at Great Bear. Mr. Cramer arranged it. Her name is Marcee Rose, and she's captain of the cheerleading team. She's taking me on a tour of the school this afternoon." He grinned. "Who knows. If she's cute, it just might be a date after all."

"Turn to page fifty-two," Jessie snapped.

"Shhhhh," the librarian warned.

Jessie moved her finger down the page. "So, what's Marcee going to show you?" she sniffed. "How to do a cartwheel? How to say 'Go, team' through a megaphone?"

"I hope she'll show me all the best places at Great Bear to party," Slater murmured.

"Oooooo, a *party* school," Jessie said. "Now, *that's* a smart way to choose your future."

"I think so," Slater said. "Your social life is an important part of your college years."

"Oh, yeah," Jessie said. "Barfing at beer bashes is so broadening."

Slater turned a page over with a loud crackle that woke up a dozing student at the end of the table. "I sure hope Marcee has a more lighthearted attitude," he said. "Then again, Attila the Hun probably has a more lighthearted attitude than Spano the Spoilsport."

"Well, excuse me for thinking that college might be a super-important preparation for the rest of your life," Jessie said angrily.

"*Shhhhhh,*" the librarian warned again.

"Great," Slater whispered back furiously. "Then college should prepare *you* to be a party-pooping old maid!"

"And it should prepare *you* to be an ignorant ex-jock buying comic books you can't even read!" Jessie said, her voice rising.

The sound of clicking heels came from behind them. "This is a place for reading," the librarian whispered to them. "If you two are going to argue, I suggest you take it outside."

"But—," Jessie said.

"*Now,*" the librarian said.

Slater closed his book with a grin. "Aw, shucks," he said. "I can't study anymore."

Jessie's lips pressed together. She was so frustrated and mad at Slater she couldn't even talk. He was being a swelled-headed, ignorant jock, and she hated him. But even worse than that, he didn't even bother to flirt with her anymore! He treated her like a friend. No, *worse* than that. He treated her like a *sister.* A pain-in-the-neck, nagging sister.

"Can you give me a ride home?" Slater asked her as they walked out of the library. "I jogged to the gym."

Jessie wanted to tell him to go ahead and jog home so that he'd be all sweaty and gross for Marcee, but she didn't. The truth was, she *wanted* to spend more time with him. Even if they argued all the way home. She almost groaned aloud. She was completely and totally pathetic!

She drove back to Slater's through the streets of Palisades. If she hadn't been driving, she would have kicked herself. Why did she have to start an argument? Just because she knew better than Slater what was good for him, did that mean she always had to tell him so?

Slater didn't say anything. But he didn't seem to be mad. He stared out the window, humming a pleasant tune. Jessie wanted to scream at him to stop sounding so happy when she was so miserable.

She pulled into Slater's driveway. She stared at her hands on the steering wheel and tried to drum up the courage to apologize. Or at least wave a white flag for a truce.

"Listen, Slater, I—"

Slater gave a low whistle. "Whoa, *momma.*"

The old, familiar warmth in his tone made color rush to her cheeks. Jessie looked up with a shy smile. But to her horror, Slater wasn't looking at her at all. He was looking over her shoulder toward his house.

Jessie turned. A petite girl was standing on Slater's lawn. She was wearing a short, pink miniskirt, little white boots, and a cropped pink-and-white-striped top. She looked like a peppermint stick, Jessie thought disgustedly. But her legs were shapely and tan, and her long, white-blond hair cascaded down her back. Jessie noted sourly that the girl looked like she was in very excellent shape. *She* wouldn't feel out of place in a gym.

The peppermint-stick girl saw the car and waved; then she bounced toward them.

"Well, if it isn't Miss Aerobics of nineteen ninety-four," Jessie snarled.

"You said it," Slater said appreciatively.

The girl came around to Slater's side of the car. "Wow, I'm really glad you drove up. Are you Albert Clifford Slater? I'm Marcee Rose. I guess I'm early. Nobody was home. Wow, I'm really glad you drove up."

"You said that," Jessie said sweetly.

"Call me A.C.," Slater said. "I'm really glad to meet you, Marcee."

"Wow, I am totally glad to meet you, too," Marcee said.

"I'm Jessie Spano," Jessie said pointedly.

"Hi," Marcee said without looking at her. "So,

like, can we get together now, A.C.? I mean, I know I'm early and everything. I don't want to interrupt, like, something." Her eyes coolly flicked over at Jessie and then warmed when they shot back to Slater. "But somehow I really don't think I am."

"It's, like, totally okay and everything," Jessie said. "I mean, I don't, like, mind at all."

Marcee's china blue eyes slid over and rested on Jessie briefly. "I'm sure," she said.

It's war, Jessie thought.

"I can't wait to show you Great Bear," Marcee said to Slater. "It's such a totally cool school."

"Let's go, Marcee," Slater said with a broad grin. He got out of the car and shut the door.

"Awesome," Jessie muttered, but nobody heard her.

Slater waggled his fingers in a short wave. "Bye, Jess. See you."

"Bye," Jessie said.

He didn't even look at her. Jessie gunned the motor and peeled out. On the way, her wheels stuck and spun in a patch of mud by Slater's driveway. A few drops of mud splattered on Marcee's little pink skirt.

Jessie stuck her head out of the car window. "Wow, I'm, like, totally sorry," she called.

"I'm sure," Marcee said.

Chapter 6

▼　▲　▼　▲　▼

Kelly sighed and pushed away her taco. "I can't even think about food," she told Zack. "All I can think about is yogurt."

"Really?" Zack asked sympathetically. He had taken a break from Intelpro to meet Kelly at the mall during her dinner break. Kelly looked exhausted, and he didn't want to burden her with his problems right off the bat.

"Yes," Kelly said, sighing again. "Sometimes I think about those little coconut flakes I sprinkle on top. And last night, I dreamed about sliced bananas." She dropped her chin in a mango-scented hand. Mango had been the flavor of the day at the Yogurt 4-U. "I hate work," she moaned.

"Me, too," Zack said. "I haven't had a chance to tell you, but—"

"And Gus doesn't make it any easier," Kelly said. "He's always yelling at me. Slice more strawberries. Open another tin of coconut. I'm putting too many M&M's on the sundaes. Meanwhile, the reason the M&M's keep disappearing is because Gus takes a handful every time he walks by!"

"That's tough, Kelly," Zack said. "But let me tell you, the problems at Intelpro are worse. Monday, Screech—"

"I only put a teaspoon of M&M's on," Kelly grumbled, pushing her bangs out of her eyes. "I *swear.*"

"He found a bug in the system," Zack said, pushing aside his own cheeseburger.

"Gus is a fanatic about bugs, too," Kelly said. "I scour that tile so much, I'm going to wear it away."

"Kelly, Screech thinks that—"

"And I'll tell you something else, Zack," Kelly said, reaching for a tortilla chip. "I know I need the money, but I don't need it this badly. I can barely take Gus three times a week. If I have to see him every day this week—"

"If we don't catch the spy—," Zack mused.

"I'll really be in trouble," they said together.

Kelly looked at Zack. Slowly, she put down her chip. "Zack, what's going on?" she asked quietly. "Something's really wrong, isn't it?"

Zack nodded. "I think it is."

She put her hand over his. "I'm sorry. I've been going on and on about my stupid problems—"

"They're not stupid," Zack said.

"Whatever," Kelly said. "I haven't been listening to you at all. Tell me."

Zack started from the beginning and told Kelly everything that had happened. Her deep blue eyes got wider and wider as he outlined how serious the situation was.

"The worst part of it—well, *almost* the worst part," Zack amended, "is that my dad is counting on me. This past month, we've really been on the same wavelength, you know? Now I've let him down again by allowing Screech to work on the software without asking him first."

"But you wouldn't have found out about the spy if you hadn't," Kelly pointed out. "You could end up *saving* your dad's company."

"I guess so," Zack said. "But I still don't think Dad will be crazy about me meddling in the first place. And, Kelly, what if we don't find the spy? Dad will be back in a few days. And he's releasing the software next week!"

"We can do it," Kelly assured him. "You were right about Screech. If there's one thing he knows, it's computers. And while he's tracking the spy through the system, we can track him down another way."

Zack looked at her. "*We?*"

Kelly grinned. "I didn't want to work double shifts at the Yogurt 4-U, anyway."

Zack squeezed her hand. "You're the greatest."

"I'll call Lisa and ask her to help, too," Kelly said, munching on a chip. "She's at loose ends this week. She blocked out all this free time to spend with Jeff, but then she found out he's got a major term paper to do. She'll be glad to help out. All she's doing is writing Jeff's name over and over in her diary."

"Great," Zack said. "I feel better already."

Kelly smiled at him reassuringly and passed him the guacamole. It was funny, Zack thought as he took a bite of his cheeseburger. Lately, things with Kelly hadn't been great. They hadn't been *bad*, exactly. But with her new interest in acting and with him spending more time with his family, they hadn't seen as much of each other. Maybe they'd both needed a little space. But as soon as he'd needed her, she was there. He'd never had to ask.

No question: His friends were the greatest. And his girlfriend was the best of all.

▲   ▼   ▲

Marcee drove Slater to Great Bear University in her little red BMW convertible.

"Daddy bought it for me for my birthday," she told Slater. "I wanted pink, but I didn't have the heart to tell him I was, like, disappointed."

"Red is pretty close," Slater said. "Think of it as a deeper shade of pink."

"That's true," Marcee breathed, as if she'd never

thought of such a thing before. "A.C., you are so smart. That's so unusual to meet a guy with your kind of bod who has brains." She cast him a sidelong look. "You are going to mow down the babes at school."

Slater couldn't help grinning at Marcee's flattery. If Jessie had been there, she'd be rolling her eyes. But it felt good to have a girl appreciate him for once. Marcee didn't notice his grades. She noticed his brain. Jessie didn't realize that there was a difference.

They got to Great Bear in practically no time at all. Marcee hopped out of the car, bubbling about all the awesome things she was going to show him.

The campus was quiet, with most of the students away on spring break. Marcee took him through the dorms, showing him the common rooms with wide-screen TVs and comfortable couches. She showed him the swimming pool, the tennis courts, the exercise rooms, and the rathskeller, where Marcee said there was "an awesome bash every Friday night." He had a cappuccino at the coffee bar and cruised some off-campus hangouts. He sat on a bench in the grassy quad where Marcee said the coolest people hung out. Then he and Marcee had a terrific late lunch in the alumni dining room, courtesy of Mr. Cramer.

Slater finished the last of his iced tea. "It was a great tour," he said to Marcee.

"Isn't it an awesome school?" Marcee agreed. "You're going to love it here, A.C. It's so much fun, you just can't believe it. I must have at least fifty best friends, I swear."

"The one thing you didn't show me was classrooms," Slater said.

"Why would you want to see those?" Marcee asked, puzzled. "They're all the same. Gosh, we'll have a great season next year with you on the team."

"Thanks," Slater said. "Actually, Marcee, I *would* like to see some classrooms. Well, not classrooms, exactly. You see, I want to major in broadcasting. Can we tour the college studio after lunch?"

Marcee frowned. "Studio? Like a dance studio?"

"No, a broadcasting studio," Slater explained. "You know: cameras, lights, equipment."

Marcee's puzzlement cleared. "Oh, sure. I know what you mean."

"Great," Slater said, putting down his napkin.

"Except we don't have one," Marcee said, dotting at her pink lips with a napkin.

"You don't have a college TV station?" Slater asked, surprised. "But Mr. Cramer said that Great Bear has a College of Broadcasting."

"Oh, sure," Marcee said. "But broadcasting majors have this special arrangement with Santa Teresa College. They can take classes there and use their equipment and stuff."

"But isn't Santa Teresa over an hour south of here?" Slater asked.

"I guess," Marcee said. "It's a real pretty road, though. My friend Dawn took a class there last semester. She's going to change majors, though. She said it was a hassle."

"I can't believe you don't have a TV station," Slater mused. "Everything here is state-of-the-art."

"Well," Marcee said, frowning in concentration, "most of the money Great Bear gets from alumni goes to sports. That's why our teams are so awesome. Did I mention that I was on the golf team?"

"Yeah," Slater said absentmindedly. He had to admit he was disappointed to find there wasn't a college station to work at. At California University, they had their own broadcast news show.

Suddenly, Marcee sat up excitedly. "Hey! I almost forgot. There's, like, a radio station on campus. It's kind of tiny and depressing, though. The guy who runs it, Stanley, is kind of weird. He plays opera a lot. Nobody listens to it. But if you want to go, just say the word, and we're there," she finished generously.

"That's okay," Slater said.

"Wow, I can see that you're really disappointed," Marcee said. "But, A.C., even if it *is* kind of a hassle to have to drive to another school to take classes, the stuff you get here is so awesome, you probably won't mind much. Really. I mean, compared to the incredible school spirit and great party atmosphere here, no school can compete." She took a sip of iced tea. "Besides, you could always change your major."

"But I don't want to do that," Slater said.

Marcee sighed. "What's the difference? You're an athlete. If you're, like, a football star, TV stations will want to hire you. They don't care about your *major.*"

"I guess you're right," Slater said slowly.

"You see?" Marcee said. "I'm smart sometimes, too."

▲   ▼   ▲

Lisa stood at the window and peeked out from behind the curtains.

"Is everyone gone, Lisa?" Zack called. It was seven-thirty at night, and Lisa, Kelly, Zack, and Screech were waiting for the offices to empty. Since Intelpro was releasing software the following week, everyone was working overtime. Some of the employees would even be working through the weekend.

"What? Oh, yeah. There's no cars in the parking lot except for ours and the security guard's. Gosh, I wonder what Jeff is doing right now."

Zack rolled his eyes at Kelly. He had been glad to have Lisa's help, but so far, he'd had to repeat everything twice in order to get her attention.

"You know what I found out today?" Zack said to Kelly. "Miles Moriarity drives a Jaguar. I think we should try and find out what his salary is. I don't think my dad pays him enough to afford such an expensive car."

"Maybe he's had it awhile," Kelly suggested.

Zack shook his head. "I can see on the window where the sticker was. Miles didn't do a very good job of soaking it off."

"Wow," Kelly said admiringly. "That's good detective work."

"Just call me Sherlock Holmes," Zack replied. "Now, while Lisa researches the employee records on Smedley's computer and Screech still tries to find out when the spy first sneaked into the system, let's check out Mr. Moriarity's office."

"Okay," Kelly said. "Good luck, Lisa."

Lisa was staring dreamily out the window.

"Lisa!" Zack rapped out.

She started guiltily. "What?"

"You said you'd call up the employee records," Zack reminded her. "Screech will show you how. Look for anything out of the ordinary, anything suspicious. Start with all the systems engineers, like Miles and Hal and Chris. I wrote their names down on a pad by the keyboard."

Lisa nodded and started out of the office. Zack and Kelly followed her, but then they turned right toward Miles Moriarity's office.

"He left the lights on," Zack said as they walked in. "Very helpful."

"What are we looking for, Zack?" Kelly asked.

"I have no idea," Zack said, picking up an appointment book and leafing through it. "But let's start looking."

Kelly examined a stack of books and then moved on to look at the items on Miles's messy desk. "Look at all these peanut shells," she said. "This guy needs a maid."

"Whoa, Kelly, listen to this," Zack said. "Miles has a lunch date every Friday with the same person, Al X. Do you think he's passing information?"

"I don't know," Kelly said. "It could be a friend."

"Mr. X? A friend? I don't think so," Zack said darkly. "It sounds like—"

Suddenly, they heard heavy footsteps coming down the hall. Zack looked out the window and, in a flash, saw Miles Moriarity's Jaguar under the trees. "Oh, my gosh!" he whispered. "It's him! It's Miles!"

"Let's get out of here," Kelly breathed.

But the footsteps were now right outside the door. There was no escape!

Chapter 7

▼   ▲   ▼   ▲   ▼

Quickly, Zack grabbed Kelly and pulled her into the tiny closet. They heard Miles Moriarity come into the office.

Crammed up next to Zack, there was enough light coming from beneath the door for Kelly to see a raincoat hanging on a hook between them. She tilted her head slightly to show it to Zack. He closed his eyes in frustration.

What if Miles had come back for his coat? It was a mild, clear night, but you never knew. Somehow, Miles seemed like the kind of nerdy guy who'd wear a raincoat even on a sunny day.

Zack wanted to kick himself, but there wasn't enough room. He had dived into the closet because he didn't want Miles to suspect that they were investigating him. But if he found them in his closet, he'd have a pretty good clue.

What reason could he give for being there? Zack wondered. *Hi, Miles. Just checking your hanger supply. Oh, Miles, hello. Just measuring executive closet space.* Or how about a simple: *Kelly and I just wanted to be alone.*

As a matter of fact, Zack thought suddenly, when was the last time he *had* been alone with Kelly? He couldn't even remember! Now she was so close, she was practically in his arms. He smelled her shampoo and her soap and felt the soft skin of her arm pressed up against him. If only Sherlock Holmes had known how much fun a female sidekick could be!

Zack heard the rustle of papers. Suddenly, Kelly's blue eyes widened in alarm as she grabbed Zack's hand. That was when Zack realized he'd taken Miles's appointment book in the closet with him.

They each held their breath as they listened to the rustle of papers. Miles cleared his throat. He whistled softly under his breath. There was the sound of a chair skidding, and he said "Ouch," as though he'd stubbed his toe.

Finally, they heard the jangle of keys. Then footsteps heading to the door. Then *click*. The lights were out.

Kelly spoke close to his ear. "Should we go?"

"Let's wait a minute," Zack whispered back.

They breathed softly together, listening to make sure Miles was gone for good. Kelly's skin glowed in the darkness. Her shiny hair fell against his wrist, and Zack got goose bumps.

"Now?" she said.

"Another minute," he said. "Just to be sure."

Kelly waited for another thirty seconds. "Now?"

Zack's lips brushed her forehead. "Mmmmm, not yet."

Kelly began to smile. "Zack—"

"We have to be completely sure, Kelly," Zack said earnestly. "And while we wait, we might as well amuse ourselves."

Kelly gave a soft giggle, which stopped when Zack bent to kiss her.

Zack lost himself in Kelly's scent and her warm, sweet kiss. It had been so long! He sighed as her slender arms reached up to encircle his neck.

Suddenly, the door banged open. Light hit their eyes, and they blinked in shock.

Lisa stood there, her hands on her hips. "Hey," she said. "No fair. I'm dateless and lonely. You guys aren't *allowed* to have fun."

Kelly grinned. "Sorry, Lisa. We were hiding from Miles."

Lisa started guiltily. "Miles? I thought he left."

"You *told* us he left," Zack said, stepping out of the closet. "Then I saw his car underneath the trees on the south side of the parking lot."

"Oh," Lisa said in a small voice. "I guess I missed it. I'm sorry, guys."

"Miles almost caught us, Lisa," Zack said. "This is serious stuff."

"I know, I know," Lisa said. "I am sorry, Zack. I'll be more careful, I promise. But listen, you guys, I found out all kinds of neat stuff."

"I did, too," Zack said. "Miles meets a guy named Mr. X every Friday."

"And Screech found out that the spy first sneaked into the system last Thursday," Lisa said. "Maybe Miles passed the information on!"

"Come on," Zack said grimly. "We have work to do."

▲   ▼   ▲

"Last Thursday night, nine P.M.," Screech said. "That's when the spy first invaded. And not only that. It happened here, on an Intelpro monitor."

"The spy *is* in the company," Kelly breathed.

"And I accessed the security book from that night," Lisa said. "Everyone has to sign in and out, and it all gets logged into the computer. Here's the list of everyone who was still here Thursday:

Miles Moriarity
Hal Torrance
Chris Ciccolini

"The usual suspects," Zack said. "All the hackers."

"Nobody signed in or out," Lisa said, staring at the list. "They ordered Chinese food and ate dinner here."

"So one of these guys is the spy," Kelly said. "Any guesses, Zack?"

"I'm still betting on Miles, but I don't know," Zack said.

Screech whirled around in his chair. "I've got my doubts about Chris," he said. "I knew I knew him from someplace. He used to work for Ernest Zeiderbaum of EZ Software Systems." Screech gazed at them triumphantly, as though this was highly significant.

"Translation, please, Screech," Kelly said. "This does not compute."

"Ernest Zeiderbaum was one of the original hackers from way back," Screech said. "One of the pioneers of cyberspace. He developed some of the most original software in the world. Companies offered him mondo bucks—millions—to work for them. There was only one problem. Ernest didn't think that anybody should have to *buy* computer software. He thought that cyberspace should be open to anyone, anytime."

"Wow," Lisa said. "Kind of like Robin Hood with a mouse."

"So what he did was, he built in all these back doors into his software programs," Screech explained. "That means that if you stumble on the right code, you can access software for free if it's on a network."

"I'm not following this," Kelly said. "I don't even know how to use a typewriter."

Screech waved his hands. "It doesn't matter, Kelly. What matters is, what if Chris 'Cruncher' Ciccolini still believes Ernest was right? What if he's sabotaging Mr. Morris's program so that he can turn around and fix the problems and offer it for free?" He shrugged. "It sounds crazy, and Ernest kind of turned out that way in the end. He's a recluse now."

Zack nodded slowly. "I see what you mean, Screech."

Lisa was staring at the computer-generated picture of Hal. "Wait a second," she said. "Isn't this the guy who broke into his school's computer and changed his grades? They called him Prince Hal Torrance because he changed the grades of the entire senior class."

Kelly walked over slowly. "Are you sure that's him? Didn't that kid go to jail?"

"Suspended sentence," Lisa said. "It's definitely him. I never forget a boy's face. I thought he was cute." Everyone stared at her. "I was younger then," she said faintly.

Zack blew out a long breath. "So Hal likes to break into systems just for the thrill of it. That means we've got a problem, folks. And it's called too many suspects. Where are we going to start?"

Everyone frowned, thinking hard. Screech tapped a pencil against the keyboard. Lisa studied her fingernails. Kelly twisted a lock of hair into a pretzel shape. Zack began to pace.

"If only we could get the spy to sneak on to the computer right when we were looking," Kelly said. "Then Screech could trace him to the right terminal."

"But how can we get him to do that?" Lisa grumbled. "We can't even let him know that we know he's around."

Zack whirled around. "You guys are right," he said triumphantly. "And I know just what we need."

"What?" the others demanded.

"To catch a rat, what do you need?" Zack asked. "A trap!"

▲   ▼   ▲

Later that night, Kelly and Lisa left Zack and Screech working out the details of their plan at the

Max. Lisa dropped Kelly off at home. Kelly yawned as she started up the walk. She was so tired. Catching a spy was even harder than squirting yogurt into little plastic dishes and asking "Would you like a topping with that?" a million times a night.

As she reached the front porch steps, she noticed that the light was out. Then she saw a tall shadow move from the corner toward her.

Kelly gasped. "Stay away from me!" she yelled in a quavering voice. "I know karate!"

She heard a familiar laugh, and the shadow turned into Jessie. "You do not, Kapowski," Jessie said. "You can barely swat a fly."

Kelly let out the breath she'd been holding. "It's you, Jessie. I thought you were the spy."

"Spy?" Jessie asked.

Quickly, Kelly explained what had been going on. "But I think we're on the right track," she said finally. "We're getting really close."

"It sounds pretty exciting," Jessie said. "Let me know if you need more help."

"We didn't want to ask you and Slater," Kelly said, settling into the glider on the porch. "We knew you were busy studying."

Jessie sighed and flopped down next to Kelly.

"I don't know about that," she said glumly. "Slater has asked me for a rain check so many times, I'm going to have to start carrying an umbrella."

"What do you mean?" Kelly asked. "I thought his grade was really important to him."

"I thought it was important to him, too," Jessie said. "But now only Marcee is."

"Who's Marcee?" Kelly asked.

"She's, like, this really, really awesome babe," Jessie said. "She goes to Great Bear University, and she's all over Slater like hot fudge on a sundae."

Kelly shuddered. "Don't mention sundaes. It reminds me of the Yogurt 4-U. How did Slater meet this girl? I thought he was busy studying with you."

"He got a four-year scholarship to Great Bear University, so he thinks he doesn't have to study," Jessie said. "They've pretty much come out and told him that they don't care what his grades are as long as he can throw a football."

"Oh," Kelly said.

"It's *wrong*, Kelly!" Jessie burst out. "Slater was never the best student in the world, but he always did his best. Now he's refusing to learn whole blocks of material, saying it's a waste of time. All of a sudden, he's turned into a lazy jerk with no goals except partying and meeting girls. I mean, that's how he's talking about college, like it's just this big stage for everyone to admire him."

"The star jock syndrome," Kelly said.

"Bingo," Jessie said gloomily. "He makes me sick. Pretty soon, his head will be so big that Goodyear will use it for a blimp."

Kelly couldn't help laughing, and Jessie joined in reluctantly.

"I could just kill him," Jessie said. "He's drooling all over Marcee, the peppermint stick. He keeps talking about his football record like he won the Nobel Prize. And the worst thing is that he's going to flunk history. What if he comes to his senses and decides he does want to go to a better college? What if he can't graduate? Mr. Loomis is one of the toughest teachers at Bayside. He's not going to just let Slater slide."

"So what can you do?" Kelly asked Jessie softly.

"Try to talk some sense into him," Jessie said. "I keep trying, and we keep arguing. But I'm not going to give up," she added fiercely. "I've got to get him to see that I'm right."

Kelly was quiet for a minute. The moon came out from under a cloud and silvered the boards of the porch. She pushed off with her feet, and the glider rocked gently.

"What?" Jessie said.

"I didn't say anything," Kelly said.

"I know," Jessie said. "But I can hear you thinking."

Kelly laughed. "Okay. I just want to ask you something. Wasn't one of the reasons that you and Slater broke up because Slater said you were always pushing him to do what *you* wanted him to do? Didn't he say that you never gave him credit?"

"It sort of sounds familiar," Jessie said gruffly.

"And didn't he say that you didn't think he was smart enough to figure out things for himself so you always jumped in and made him feel stupid?"

"Well," Jessie said. "Maybe." She drew her knees up and hugged them. "I'm an awful person, aren't I," she moaned.

"No, you're not," Kelly said, laughing. "You're the best friend anybody could have. And most of the time, you *do* know the right thing to do because— let's face it—you *are* really smart." She turned to face Jessie. "But, Jessie, you have to understand that sometimes that just doesn't do anybody any good."

"Why not?" Jessie asked.

"Because people have to figure stuff out on their own," Kelly said. "That's the only way they really learn. You know that, Jessie."

"Sure," Jessie said. "But Slater is just so *thick* sometimes."

"I know," Kelly said. "But don't you love him, anyway? He gets swept up into stuff. He gets so enthusiastic that he can lose perspective. It's what makes him so much fun to be around."

"Tell me about it," Jessie agreed.

"But, Jessie, Slater's got a good head on his shoulders. He'll figure things out. You've got to let him learn his own lessons."

"He *won't* learn his lessons!" Jessie said. "He won't study, the dork!"

"I don't mean his *history* lessons," Kelly said. "I mean his *life* lessons. The kind of lessons you learn the hard way."

"So what are you saying, Kelly?" Jessie said. She searched Kelly's face in the moonlight. "What's your advice?"

"I mean this in the nicest way possible," Kelly told her friend. "Jessie, just shut up."

Chapter 8

▼　▲　▼　▲　▼

Thursday morning, Zack stopped on the way to Intelpro and bought a box of doughnuts. There was nothing like junk food to get the hackers to come running. He put the box by the coffee machine and waited.

Sure enough, by nine-thirty, Hal and Chris were there, their mouths full while they had their daily argument. Miles ambled in and chose a chocolate-covered doughnut rolled in peanuts.

Zack poured himself another cup of coffee and sipped it slowly. If he had any more caffeine, he'd start orbiting the planet. He'd been checking back at the coffee machine every fifteen minutes since eight-thirty.

"Listen up, lame-o," Chris was saying to Hal. "I am Cruncher the Magnificent. I'm the expert."

"I've been eating at Jumbo Jethro's since before you were born, geekoid," Hal said, chewing furiously on a cruller. "I'm telling you, their double cheeseburger deluxe is one hundred times better than Burger Heaven's."

"You have the taste buds of a *dork* deluxe," Cruncher responded, calmly pouring himself a splash more coffee to wash down his cinnamon doughnut. "Burger Heaven is numero uno, el kooketroid."

Zack wished that they'd both stop arguing so he could drop his information subtly into the conversation, but he was beginning to think that Cruncher and Hal lived to argue. Just as Zack was about to give up, Miles saved him by saying hello.

"Hi," Zack said quickly. "How's it going?"

"Uh, okay," Miles said. From somewhere deep inside his genius brain, he summoned up the correct polite response. "And how, uh, are you doing?"

"Great," Zack said loudly, so that he could penetrate Hal and Chris's conversation. "Screech is almost finished running his virus protection program."

Miles took a sip of hot coffee and winced. Behind him, Hal and Chris actually stopped arguing to listen.

"Ow," Miles said, touching his lip. "Hot. The product integrity department already ran a bunch of tests on the system. They just finished on Tuesday. Screech is just going over the same ground."

"Not really," Zack said. "He's running a whole new test just as an extra precaution. My dad wanted Screech to do it."

Hal edged closer. "How's it work?"

"When's he going to run it?" Chris asked.

Great. He had their interest. But he didn't know if they were interested because they were interested in *anything* having to do with computers, or because they wanted to foil the detection system.

"Don't ask me how it works," Zack said, waving his hand. "But Screech is brilliant when it comes to this stuff. He's going to run it tonight, after hours, so it won't interfere with anybody's work. Then we'll pick up the results tomorrow morning."

"Let me know how it goes," Miles said absentmindedly, and walked out.

Pretty casual act, Zack thought. *Was it just a ploy to escape detection?*

"Me, too," Hal said. "I designed our system. Tell your buddy to come by and we'll interface."

"Sure," Zack said, as Hal walked out.

"Never mind interfacing with that dweebathon," Chris said loudly so that Hal would overhear. "Tell him to drop by my office." Smirking, he followed Hal out the door.

Zack took another sip of coffee. It was cold. But he grinned as he tossed it down the sink.

Snap! The trap was laid.

▲   ▼   ▲

That night in the library, Jessie gritted her teeth and smiled when Slater showed up ten minutes late.

"Sorry," he said. "I was talking to Marcee on the phone. She's going to pick me up later."

That should be a new experience for her. She's probably never been to a library before.

Jessie wanted to say it, but she didn't. She just smiled wider. "Great. Want to get started?"

She passed over her notes to Slater. She'd written out a list of questions for him to look up, and he read them, frowning.

"I don't need to study the Bill of Rights," he murmured to her. "It's boring and complicated. I'll just skip that part."

Fine. It's not like the Bill of Rights is an important part of the Constitution.

Jessie thought it, but she didn't say it. It killed her, but she just nodded pleasantly.

"It's your decision," Jessie said. "Let's work on the other questions."

Slater looked surprised, but he took out his pen and began to work. He actually concentrated this time, and Jessie was impressed at how quickly he picked up the material. Time flew by. Soon it was time for Slater to meet Marcee outside.

Slater slipped into his denim jacket. "Hey, that wasn't too bad," he said.

Jessie gathered the books and stuck the pens into her purse. "You did well today," she said.

"Ooh, it sounds like you believe I just might have a half a brain after all," Slater teased as they walked toward the door.

"Oh, at least half a brain, I'd say," Jessie said, grinning. "Maybe even two-thirds."

Slater's brown eyes widened in surprise. He'd been expecting a zinger. But Jessie's grin was infectious, and he couldn't help smiling back.

"Yoo-hoo!"

Slater spun around. Marcee was waving to him from the front door. She walked toward them, her blond hair bouncing. She looked so bright and . . . pink, Slater thought. The kind of girl who just didn't belong in the library.

He stood, waiting nervously for Jessie to make a crack about his bubblegum date. But Jessie only stood there, waiting for Marcee to walk over. What had happened to his acid-tongued ex-sweetie? Had she taken a *nice* pill? Or had some body snatcher come along and substituted some other brilliant, curly-haired knockout for Jessie? Because this new Jessie did something that the old Jessie never did. She kept her mouth shut.

"Hi, Marcee," Jessie said pleasantly. "It's nice to see you again."

Whoa, Slater thought. *There's definitely a body snatcher thing happening here.*

"Hi," Marcee said shortly. "So are you finished booking it, A.C.?" She looked around at the people looking up titles in the card catalog, clicking away at computers, and hurrying by with armloads of books. "Can we split? This place, like, gives me the creeps."

Slater winced in anticipation. He waited for Jessie's response. Something like: "Yes, it has that effect on brainless types." Or: "Don't worry, Marcee—intelligence isn't contagious."

But Jessie only smiled. "I have to run, too. You kids have fun!" She waved and walked away, her long legs striding purposefully out the front door.

Slater frowned as Jessie stepped outside and took a deep breath of the warm night air. What was going on? he wondered.

Marcee tugged at his sleeve. "Come on, egghead," she said with a giggle. "Let's start having fun. This place is deadsville."

As they got outside, Jessie was chugging out of the parking lot in her mother's Toyota. She waved again and smiled.

Then it hit him. He knew what was wrong.

Jessie didn't care about him anymore.

It was impossible. But it had to be true. She was over him!

▲   ▼   ▲

Zack knew that Mrs. Smedley had keys to all the exit doors in her desk. He lifted a key to the door that led to the delivery entrance. Then, later that evening, right before he and Screech signed out, he unlocked the door. He and Screech drove out of the parking lot, down the street, and parked the car around the block.

Kelly and Lisa were waiting. The four circled back and sneaked into the delivery entrance. They closed the door behind them, and Zack locked it.

"Okay, let's go upstairs," he whispered.

The halls were dark and quiet, and the office doors hung open, giving a glimpse of shadowy interiors.

"Gosh, this is kind of spooky," Lisa whispered.

They tiptoed into Mr. Morris's office. Screech went right to the computer and turned it on. He quickly typed in some commands.

"Now what do we do?" Kelly whispered.

"Wait," Screech said.

They didn't want to turn on a light or the TV in case the security guard went by during his rounds. The only light came from the amber glow of the computer screen. Zack sat on the floor next to Kelly, watching the blinking screen. Screech's program just had to work!

If the spy signed on to the system, the computer

would beep Screech. Screech was guessing that the spy would try to cover his tracks. There was a way to hide what monitor he'd be using, Screech had explained to them. Screech would have to crack the spy's code to discover where he was.

The trick was to do it without the spy finding out. Zack didn't understand the details and didn't even try. He just crossed his fingers and prayed. He couldn't let his father's dream go down the tubes!

"Lisa's right," Kelly murmured by his side. "This *is* kind of spooky. This spy won't be dangerous, will he?"

Zack thought about Hal or Miles or Cruncher coming toward him trailing doughnut crumbs or peanut shells. "No way," he said, slipping his hand into hers and squeezing it.

"Good," she said, relieved.

But the darkness and quiet seemed to grow, and for the first time, Zack wondered how desperate the spy might be. Just because Hal and Chris seemed like a pair of quarrelsome nerds didn't mean that they couldn't be reckless or violent or even crazy. Even mild-mannered Miles might have a desperate side. A person would *have* to be desperate to take these kinds of chances, Zack thought. They were doing something illegal. They could go to jail.

This wasn't a game. And the person who was playing it wasn't fooling around. He was serious and smart and determined.

And maybe dangerous.

Zack shivered.

"Are you cold?" Kelly whispered.

"I'm fine," Zack said bravely. There was no way he'd wimp out in front of Kelly.

Beep!

Screech spun around in his chair. "He's on!" he cried.

Chapter 9

▼　▲　▼　▲　▼

Zack sprang to his feet. "Where is he?" he said, rushing over to stand behind Screech at the terminal.

Screech was frantically clicking keys. "Reserve nodes," he muttered.

"English, please," Zack demanded.

"I don't know where he is," Screech said. "I'm trying to find out. Think of it like the police tracing a call."

Zack paced impatiently. It was hard not to *move*, not to run somewhere and catch the criminal. But there was nothing to do but wait while Screech worked his binary magic.

Finally, just when Zack thought he was going to explode, Screech hit a key and yelped.

"*Gotcha!*" he crowed.

"Where, Screech?" Zack asked frantically.

Screech looked back at them, his face ghostly in the amber light. "Right down the hall," he whispered. "It's Hal's terminal."

"I knew it!" Lisa said.

"Let's go," Zack said tersely, and he took off. Kelly and Lisa were at his heels and Screech was a distant third as they headed for Hal's office.

It was too late. The room was empty.

"Hey, look," Lisa said. "His computer is on."

The gang filed in and stared at the computer screen. A single symbol shone at them, glowing amber against the black screen:

;-)

"That rat!" Screech cried. He slammed his hand down on the desk.

Zack, Lisa, and Kelly looked at him, puzzled. "What is it, Screech?" Zack asked.

"It's a signal," Screech said. His wiry curls seemed to vibrate with frustration and fury. "That big, fat rat!"

"If this is a message, I don't get it," Lisa said, peering at the screen. "What's so awful about a semicolon, a hyphen, and half a parenthesis?"

"It's a kind of informal computer language,"

Screech explained. "Turn your head to the left and read the message sideways. You'll get it."

"It's a face," Kelly said.

"And it's winking," Zack said.

"Exactly," Screech said.

"The rat is *taunting* us," Zack said slowly. "He's daring us to catch him!"

"That means he knows we're on to him," Kelly said.

"And it means he knew we'd come running to Hal's computer," Lisa added in a dire tone.

The gang exchanged worried glances.

"And it means he's smarter than we thought," Zack said.

"And maybe it means he's smarter than we are," Screech said.

Suddenly, Kelly bent down and picked something off the carpet. She held it up. It was a peanut shell.

"Maybe not," Zack said.

▲   ▼   ▲

Slater couldn't help it. His mind kept wandering. Marcee was a definite dish, but tonight, all he could think about was Jessie. It wasn't that he was thinking about her in a romantic way. He was thinking about her in an *exasperated* way.

At least Marcee didn't notice that he was distracted. First they went to a crowded dance club with loud music. Then they went to a noisy café for sodas. Then Marcee suggested a stop at a nearby carnival. By this time, Slater would have given anything for a little silence. Didn't Marcee ever want to just *talk*?

"I don't know, Marcee," he said. "A carnival sounds pretty noisy. I don't think my ears can take it."

"'Kay," Marcee said. "How about the movies? There's a late show of *Gunrunners III*."

"Besides," Slater said, "I really have to do some studying tonight. I have another session with Jessie tomorrow."

"What are you worried about? You're going to Great Bear next year. Besides," she pouted, "it's super early. I can't possibly go home before eleven o'clock. It's a *rule*."

Slater nodded. "Okay. How about a walk on the pier?"

Marcee shrugged. "That sounds, like, relaxing for sure. 'Kay."

The pier was only a few blocks from the café. They walked to it along the beach. The waves lapped gently at the shore, and the moon was a sliver in the black sky. Right now, Jessie would probably be quoting some stupid poem at him, Slater thought. It wasn't really fair of him to think that, because whenever Jessie quoted something to him, he had to admit it was usually pretty neat.

But it made him feel better to remember how different he and Jessie were. They were complete opposites. Marcee was definitely more his type. It was amazing that he and Jessie had ever been boyfriend and girlfriend at all. If they hadn't laughed so much when they were together, they would have found out sooner how incompatible they were.

"You can't fool me, A.C.," Marcee said as they reached the pier and started to stroll out over the black water. "You're distracted or something."

"Maybe I am a little bit," Slater admitted.

"Are you thinking about how totally cool it will be when we're both at the same school?" Marcee said.

"Well, no," Slater admitted. "Actually, I was thinking of something else."

"Whoa, flashing red light," Marcee said, holding up a hand. "I get it. Like, *finally*. It's a girl, isn't it?"

"Well, yes and no," Slater said. "I mean, it's a girl I *used* to go with. I don't anymore."

"Whoa, I am getting the most incredible insight right now," Marcee said. "Is it that girl you're always with? The tall one? Jeri?"

"Jessie," Slater said. "Yeah, it is."

"You know, I am, like, an incredibly good listener," Marcee said. "All my friends say so. So if you want to do some ex-girlfriend bashing, I'm here."

"That's really nice of you, Marcee," Slater said.

Usually, girls *hated* it when you talked about other girls. He knew that Jessie did.

Except today, Slater thought morosely. Today, she hadn't been bothered by Marcee at all.

"So." Marcee nudged him. "Talk."

So Slater talked. He told Marcee all about his relationship with Jessie. Of course, he couldn't begin to describe how much fun it was sometimes and how awful it was other times, but he did his best. The trouble was that every time he remembered something bad, he remembered that something good had either come out of it or had happened right afterward. Marcee kept steering him back to the bad parts, since that was where she said she could really get some good insights, so Slater tried to concentrate and remember every single terrible fight he and Jessie had had.

"Wow," Marcee said. "That's a lot of fights."

"That's the *condensed* version," Slater said.

Marcee pressed two fingers to her forehead. "'Kay. This is what I'm thinking right now. This girl is totally wrong for you."

"She is?" Slater asked. "I mean, *I* know she is. But how do *you* know she is?"

"Because *A,* you have no interests in common," Marcee said. "She hates football, she doesn't like to work out, and she likes to read all the time."

"Not *all* the time—"

"Whatever. What I'm saying is, she's crunchy granola and you're . . . well, you're definitely more along the sizzling fajita lines. You get me? Oh, and B—and this is most important—she doesn't appreciate you. No way. She keeps trying to change you all the time. I mean, really. Who does she think she is?"

"She's not that bad—"

"I'm not saying she's *bad*. I'm saying that even though she's, like, smart, she's dumb. Here she has this incredibly handsome, fun, fabu guy, and she's trashing him. I ask you."

"So why does it bother me that she doesn't care anymore?" Slater asked Marcee. "Maybe I still care about her."

"No way, babe," Marcee said. "The reason it bothers you is just because your ego can't handle it. Now, I don't blame you one teensy bit, because you are a totally buff dude and it's weird that your ex isn't pining away. But, like, get over it. Like the old expression says, move on. You deserve better, A.C."

Marcee moved closer to Slater. Her platinum hair shone silver in the moonlight. Her eyelashes fluttered over her baby blue eyes.

"Because I for one think you're incredible," she breathed. "I feel, like, lucky that you chose me to date."

Marcee was right, Slater thought. Jessie *didn't* deserve him. And here was a girl who was gorgeous and nice and who never put him down. A girl who thought she was lucky to be with him. A guy would have to be crazy not to go for that.

"Forget what's-her-name," Marcee said. "Isn't it time you had some uncomplicated fun for a change?"

She slipped her arms around his neck to bring his face down close to hers, and she kissed him.

Slater kissed her back. And Marcee was right. It *was* nice to have uncomplicated fun for a change.

▲   ▼   ▲

The first thing Friday morning, Zack went to Miles Moriarity's office. He found him running a program on his computer and absentmindedly doodling on a pad.

"Hi, Miles," Zack said, standing in the doorway.

Miles's pen scratched down the page. "Oh, Zack. Hi."

"How's it going?" Zack said.

"Uh, okay," Miles said. He sounded nervous. But he always sounded nervous, Zack thought in despair.

"So," Zack said, "did you see that great documentary on chaos theory last night on TV?"

"I must have missed it," Miles said.

"Didn't get home in time?"

"What time was it, uh, on?"

"Nine o'clock," Zack said.

"I was home," Miles said. "But I missed it, anyway."

"That's a really cool car," Zack said.

"Thanks."

"Have you had it long?" Zack asked casually.

"Not too long," Miles said. Suddenly, he looked wary. "Why?"

"No reason. I was just wondering," Zack said. "I mean, it's a really expensive car." He wandered over to the window. "Are you free for lunch today?"

"Sorry," Miles said. "I'm not."

"Oh," Zack said. "Who are you having lunch with?"

Suddenly, Screech appeared in the hallway right behind Miles's head. He motioned to Zack frantically. Zack frowned.

Screech waved his hands in the air. Miles turned and saw him.

"Wow, what a big fly," Screech said brightly. "I almost got him."

"Nice talking to you, Miles," Zack said. He left the office and followed Screech down the hall. "What's with you?" he asked him irritably.

"Kelly just called. She did some more investigating on Miles Moriarity," Screech said.

"And?"

"He's one of the Denver Moriaritys," Screech said. "They have an oil company and about twelve trillion dollars."

"Oh," Zack said. "I guess he can afford the Jaguar. And it doesn't seem like he'd spy for money. That doesn't give him much of a motive. Hey, maybe his family cut him off."

"Nope," Screech said. "Kelly said his wife just had a baby. The Moriartys are delighted. Gave little Andrew Moriarity a million-dollar trust fund just to start."

"What about the peanut shell Kelly found?"

"Miles is in and out of Hal and Cruncher's office all the time," Screech said. "Not to mention that Hal is just as much of a junk food freak as Miles is."

"The shell could have dropped there anytime, I guess," Zack admitted. "What about lunch with Mr. X?"

"His wife's name is Alex," Screech said. "Al-x, remember? You must have read it wrong."

"Oh," Zack said. "I feel like an idiot."

"I know the feeling, Zack," Screech said. "I have it all the time. But, listen, you're just really freaked out about your dad losing the company."

"I guess I just wanted to pin it on somebody," Zack agreed. "But I have to be more careful. Okay, where to now?"

"Well, we have another suspect," Screech said. "When I got here this morning, our spy was already on-line. He was trashing my virus protection program."

"He was?"

"It's okay. I have it on backup disk," Screech said, waving his hand. "But I *did* manage to trace the terminal again. It was Chris's this time!"

"Cruncher," Zack said. "He did work for that weird guy, that Ernest—"

"Zeiderbaum. Right," Screech said. "So what's our next move?"

"I think it's time for some legwork," Zack said decidedly. "And when it comes to legwork, I know just who to ask."

"Who?" Screech asked. "A private detective?"

Zack shook his head. "The best pair of legs at Bayside High."

▲   ▼   ▲

"Ready, Kelly?" Zack asked.

She nodded. "Ready."

They were standing by the water fountain at Burger Heaven. Chris had just ordered his dinner and was sitting down around the corner.

"Don't take any chances," Zack reminded her. "I just want you to talk to the guy."

Kelly peeked around the corner at Chris. "He looks pretty harmless to me," she said. "Your common, everyday kind of geek."

"Well, he might be your common, everyday master spy kind of geek," Zack said. "So be careful."

Kelly nodded.

"And remember," Zack muttered, "these guys have zero social life. Be gentle or he might pass out."

Smoothing her flowered miniskirt, Kelly headed for Chris's table. He was munching his way through a double order of fries and two Holy Cows, Burger Heaven's deluxe cheeseburger with special dressing.

"Are they any good?" Kelly said, pointing to the Holy Cows.

Chris stopped chewing and looked at her. His eyes widened, and he started to choke.

"Oh, I'm sorry," Kelly said, flustered. "Can I get you some water?"

Chris took a sip of soda. "I'm okay," he croaked. "Were you talking to *me*?"

Kelly nodded. "I was wondering if you liked your meal. I usually go to Jumbo Jethro's for his Hillbilly Cheeseburger Deluxe."

Chris nodded sadly. "I know other people who've made that mistake."

Kelly gave him a penetrating glance. "Hey, wait a second. I know you. Don't I? You used to work for Ernest Zeiderbaum. You're Chris Ciccolini."

Chris nodded bashfully. "Call me Cruncher. How do you remember Ernest? You're a little young."

"It's just that I admire hackers so much," Kelly said, sliding into the booth. "The whole hacker ethic. It's very sixties. You know, how anyone can play—any race, creed, gender, age—as long as they're good. You guys were like techno-pioneers, boldly going where no one had gone before."

"It's true," Chris said, his eyes misting over. "Want a french fry?"

Kelly smiled and bit into one delicately. "And that Ernest Zeiderbaum! I really think he was cool. All information should be free. That's *radical*."

Chris scowled. "Sure, it was a good idea. In theory."

Kelly leaned closer. "Don't you *still* think all software should be free, Cruncher?"

Chris downed a sip of soda. "Are you crazy? I'd be out of a job."

"But these are your principles!" Kelly said.

"Not anymore," Chris said. "I'm saving for a BMW. And wherever Ernest is now—I hear he's either in Portland or Bora Bora—*he's* probably driving an old pickup."

Kelly leaned back, disappointed. It looked like Chris didn't have a motive, either. If he was telling the truth.

Chris looked at her slyly. "If you're really interested in computers, maybe you'd like to see my setup. I work right down the road."

"You do? Wow. How about that," Kelly said, stalling. She still wanted to quiz Chris about his alibi. Would Zack want her to follow this through?

The offices were empty this time of night. But Zack would follow her. She'd be perfectly safe. "That would be fantastic," she said enthusiastically.

▲   ▼   ▲

It was the smell of the sizzling fries that got to Zack. He was hungry. He hadn't had dinner yet. Kelly was sitting across from Chris, chatting away. She bit into a french fry. How dare she eat when he was starving!

Zack dug into the pocket of his jeans and counted out the coins. What could it hurt? He'd only be in line for a minute or so.

But when he took his first satisfied bite of fries and looked over, Kelly was gone!

Chapter 10

▼　▲　▼　▲　▼

Zack jumped so violently that his fries shot out of the package and spilled down the neck of an older woman biting into her Holy Cow.

"Hey!" she protested. "I didn't order those!"

But he was already running, dodging a three-year-old with a fistful of apple turnover, jumping over a stroller, and dancing past a couple trying to find a table.

He ran out into the parking lot. There was no sign of Chris Ciccolini's battered red Escort.

"Kelly!" Zack shouted. But she was gone.

Had Chris discovered that Kelly was pumping him for information? Or did he just want to spend more time with a pretty girl? Zack prayed it was the second scenario. This was all his fault!

Where had they gone? he wondered frantically. He had no idea where Chris lived. Zack would have to run back to the office and access the employee records. He should have done that in the first place, Zack thought, groaning aloud. He should have been prepared for anything. Now he would lose precious time going back to the office and . . .

The office. Where else would a hacker take a girl he was trying to impress? For a hacker, his computer was the equivalent of moonlight and roses.

Zack jumped in his Mustang and took off. Kelly was probably okay, he told himself. They weren't even sure that Chris Ciccolini was the spy. And even if he *was,* that didn't mean he'd figure out that Kelly was trying to trap him.

Unless she asked one too many questions . . .

Zack roared into the parking lot and pulled up by the front door. He signed in with a scrawl and saw Chris's signature above his. "And guest" was written next to it.

Zack took the stairs two at a time. The hallway was dark. There was a shaft of light coming from Chris's office.

"I'll get you now, you double-dealing traitor!" Chris bellowed.

"No, Cruncher!" Kelly squealed. "Don't!"

Zack burst into the office. Chris was bending over Kelly, his large, stocky body blocking her from view. Zack vaulted across the office and tackled him. Chris went down with an *oof.*

"Zack!" Kelly screamed, springing up. "What are you doing?"

Zack looked up at her from his position on top of Chris. "What are you talking about? I'm saving your life!"

"What are *you* talking about!" Kelly said. "Chris was showing me a video game."

"Oh," Zack said in a small voice.

"I was winning, too," Kelly said.

"Would you mind," Chris gasped, "getting off me now?"

Zack got off him and stood up. Grunting, Chris raised himself up. He checked his arms and legs.

"Nothing's broken," he said. "Hey, I didn't know she was your girlfriend, Zack."

"It's okay," Zack mumbled.

Kelly sighed. "I think we should tell him what's going on, Zack. He has an ironclad alibi. He told me how he faxes his food orders in, and I asked him to give me an example, like for last Thursday night, and he punched it up on the computer. He and Hal ordered a pizza and ate it with Miles. They *all* have alibis. The fax is timed, and so is the pizza's arrival. The pizza place faxes them back when it's ready, just to let them know to come downstairs to pick it up."

Chris looked from one to the other. "What's

going on?" he asked suspiciously. He squinted at Kelly. "You were conning me, weren't you? I knew it. I knew it was too good to be true. I'll *never* have a date on Friday night!"

Kelly smiled. "I'm really sorry, Cruncher. I did enjoy talking to you." She looked at Zack. "Maybe he can help us."

Zack nodded. He turned to Chris. "You'd better have a seat."

"This is serious, isn't it?" Chris said.

Zack nodded. "It concerns the future of Intelpro."

Chris dropped his head in his hands. "There goes my BMW," he moaned.

▲   ▼   ▲

On Saturday, Slater had promised to do Coach Sonski a favor. The freshman football team had ended up in the bottom of the ranking that year, and some of the players had been overheard threatening to quit. The coach had thought that a pep talk from his favorite player would help, and he'd asked Slater to come by and give an informal talk after their last scrimmage of the year.

Slater drove to Bayside High and parked near the gym entrance. He hadn't prepared anything to say. He had figured he'd just wing it. He'd probably heard hundreds of pep talks from his years of being in sports. He wasn't worried a bit.

The familiar smell of the gym hit his nostrils. Probably Jessie would think it was gross, but Slater loved the smell of steam and sweat. It made him think of wins and losses and grim determination.

Marcee would understand, Slater decided as he headed down the hall. She was a sports nut, like he was. He was glad he'd met the right girl at last.

He pushed open the door to the football locker room. The team members were sitting around on the benches. Most of them were slumped over in various attitudes of boredom and let's-get-this-over-with. *Tough crowd*, Slater thought.

Coach Sonski motioned him forward. "You all know A. C. Slater," he told the team. "He played four incredible seasons for Bayside High. He'd like to say a few words to you today."

Slater went to the front of the room. The faces looked up at him. Someone suppressed a yawn. Someone else was playing a handheld video game. Slater could feel perspiration begin to tickle the back of his neck. Why hadn't he prepared anything?

Slater hesitated. He couldn't give them the standard pep talk. He'd have to take a different approach.

"Hi, guys," he said easily, in a quiet, conversational tone. "I know you've probably heard a hundred pep talks since you started playing sports. I know I have. Coach Sonski gives the best ones. All about how you have to play your heart out on the field. How you have to give your all for the team. And the coach is right about all those things. But today, instead of talking about what you can bring *to* football, I want to talk about what you can take away. What the game can give to you, not what you give to the game."

He grinned. "I hate to bring up the word *lessons* during spring break, but I've learned a bunch of lessons from football. And it's not about how to date the cutest cheerleaders."

The team laughed. Some of them straightened up. He was winning them over.

"Life isn't fair," Slater said. "Sometimes you do your best and it's not good enough. Sometimes you try your hardest and you don't win. But football taught me something. What matters is the trying. Even if we lost, if I played my best game, I felt okay. But if we won, and I played lousy, I'd kick myself all the way home. And I deserved it.

"Look," Slater continued. "I'm not going to stand here and tell you that losing is fun. It isn't. It hurts. Sometimes it's embarrassing. It doesn't get you the best girls or the slaps on the back on Monday mornings. But sometimes you get something just as good. Something important. And that shows you're doing something for the love of it. Once you start thinking that way, you stop being lazy. You stop being sloppy. You give one hundred and ten percent, one hundred and ten percent all of the time. It isn't easy. But it's what the game demands. And if you don't respect that, you don't respect the game."

Slater leaned forward. Every eye was on him now. "You know what?" he said. "I'm going to make you a promise. Once you do that, once you decide to give your all no matter what, things start to happen. What happens on the field spills over into your life. You start making better choices. You start not giving up just because something's hard."

The earnestness in the boys' eyes in front of him gave Slater a sudden jolt. Suddenly, he wasn't just talking. He was *listening.* And he felt like a fraud.

What had he been doing but coasting? What had he been doing but being sloppy and lazy? He wasn't giving one hundred and ten percent this week. He wasn't even giving fifty percent. He was coasting because it was easy. He was being just plain dumb.

"Once you start to realize that trying can be an art form, just like winning," Slater finished, "you've got it made."

He stopped. At first, the team just sat there. They'd never had a pep talk that didn't end with something like ". . . so get out on that field and kick some butt!" But once they realized Slater's talk was over, they burst into applause.

Slater held up a hand. "Thanks, guys. Now I have to get going. It's time to follow my own advice."

He shook Coach Sonski's hand and hurried back to the parking lot. He drove home, thinking about Jessie. She'd been right. He *had* been a jerk. But he wasn't about to tell her so. Marcee was right, too. Jessie had blown it with him for good.

When he drove up to his house, he was surprised to see Marcee's red convertible in the driveway.

"Hi," she said, running up to him. She was wearing a little tennis dress and swinging a racket. "Your mom said I could wait. I've just got to have a good set of tennis." She reached into the car and rested her hand on his arm. "And I bet with those muscles, you can give me a really good workout."

Slater got out of the car. "Sorry, Marcee. I can't. I have to study." He looked at his watch. "As a matter of fact, Jessie will be here any minute."

"Wait," Marcee said. "Like, hold the phone. You're going to *study* on a beautiful Saturday? Come on," she wheedled. "Come with me."

"Marcee, really, I—"

Suddenly, she threw her arms around him. She looked up into his face. "Don't you remember last night?" she cooed. "I'll never, ever forget it."

Slater heard the sound of a throat clearing behind him. Somehow, he knew just who it would be.

"Sorry to interrupt," Jessie said. "You look kind of busy."

"I was just talking A.C. into a game of tennis," Marcee said. She didn't drop her arms from around his neck. "A growing boy needs his exercise."

"He sure does," Jessie said cheerfully. "If you want to fit in some tennis, Slater, it's no problem. We can get together later."

"You see?" Marcee told him. "It'll be fun. Really."

Slater stared straight into Jessie's hazel eyes. They were clear and bright. She wasn't mad. She wasn't jealous. She wasn't even *peeved,* or *irritated,* or *mildly annoyed.* He knew Jessie. She could never hide her feelings. She just didn't care about him anymore.

"You sure you wouldn't mind?" he said.

"Mind?" Jessie smiled. "Of course not."

▲   ▼   ▲

Jessie felt her cheeks. The smile was still plastered on her face, even though Marcee's little red car had disappeared around the corner.

She massaged her cheeks to make her face return to normal. She'd never thought it would be so hard to be . . . well, *nice.*

But the worst part, she thought, slinging her backpack over her shoulder and trudging toward home, was that it wasn't working. She and Slater weren't fighting, sure. But he was seeing more and more of Marcee. And *more* of her was exactly what he *was* seeing, Jessie thought, disgruntled. If that tennis dress had been any shorter, Marcee would be wearing it as a necklace.

She had to keep her cool, no matter what it cost her. She had to show Slater that she could change, just for him. Sooner or later, he'd come to his senses.

Or she'd knock Marcee into the ozone.

Whichever came first.

▲　　▼　　▲

On Sunday afternoon, Zack, Screech, Kelly, and Lisa headed for the Intelpro offices. Some of the staff would also be pulling overtime that day, since the software expo started the next week.

Everybody was yawning as they drove into the parking lot. "Thanks for coming here again," Zack told the gang. "I know it's getting to be a real drag."

"I have the feeling we're going to crack this case today," Screech said.

"We have to," Zack said. "Dad is coming back tomorrow morning. He checked out that rumor in San Francisco and it turned out not to be true at all."

"Hmmm," Kelly said as they walked to the building. "I wonder if someone planted the rumor to get your dad out of town."

"It's a thought," Zack said. "I bet you're right, Kelly."

"My timing is getting better and better," Screech said. "Last night, I came really close to catching the spy."

"What happened?" Lisa asked. She had left early to meet Jeff at the Max.

"We ran to the monitor," Zack said. "This time, it was some guy in product services."

"Only there was a crumpled Holy Cow wrapper there," Kelly said.

"Cruncher!" Lisa breathed.

"It was just to throw us off the scent," Zack said.

"And it didn't work," Kelly said.

"Yeah," Screech agreed. "That wrapper *still* smelled like onions."

They walked down the hall to Mr. Morris's office. It was an overcast day, and the place was dusky and gloomy. Zack didn't even bother switching on the light.

"I'm so tired," he said. "I could just lie down and take—*yeeeeooooww!*"

"Zack?" Kelly switched on the light. Zack was lying on the floor where the couch used to be. Boxes of files were lined up on the gray industrial carpet. Mr. Morris's computer was sitting on the floor. All of the furniture was gone!

Chapter 11

▼　▲　▼　▲　▼

"What happened to the furniture?" Kelly asked, startled.

"How could it disappear like that? It was gorgeous," Lisa said, looking around.

"It must have been the spy," Zack said, rubbing his elbow. "But why?"

"Maybe it wasn't the spy," Lisa said. "Maybe it was the guy in charge of office supplies."

"Oh, Zack," Kelly said. "Could you have forgotten to pay a bill or something? You *have* been concentrating on catching the spy."

Zack groaned. "Oh, no. Can anything else go wrong? Dad will be back tomorrow!"

"Screech, is there any way you can check this out?" Lisa asked.

"Sure," Screech said. He balanced the computer monitor on a box and began to type. "Do you know who was in charge of ordering?" he asked Zack.

"Mrs. Smedley, I think," Zack said.

Screech tapped a few keys. After a moment, he spoke up. "This is funny. Mrs. Smedley ordered the stuff from Acme Office Furniture's start-up line. But the invoice says that Acme delivered furniture from its deluxe line. That's twice as expensive."

"I thought that furniture was too nice," Zack said.

Screech clicked a few more keys. "This is even weirder. There are *two* orders here. One order is for furniture from the deluxe line and that was delivered to Intelpro. The other order for cheaper furniture got saved in the computer *before* the order for the good stuff was made, but it looks like it was never actually delivered. Meanwhile, Zack sent the bill for the less expensive furniture to the accounting department. In other words, the company paid less than half of what it should have. So Acme came along and repossessed the furniture."

"We have to fix this," Zack said. "Today."

"What about the spy?" Lisa asked.

"We have to do both," Zack said. "And I bet you the spy is behind this. It's a diversion. We have to get to the bottom of it. Screech, can you trace who sent the order to the furniture company?"

Screech frowned. "There's a code here, but maybe I can figure it out." He turned and looked at them. "Especially if I have some junk food."

"Great idea," Lisa said. She reached for one of the takeout menus on the floor. "Do you want pizza or chow mein?"

Suddenly, Kelly sat up. "Wait a second. Say that again."

"Pizza or chow mein?" Lisa asked.

"Exactly," Kelly said.

"Okay," Screech said. "Pizza or chow mein."

Kelly looked at Zack. "Zack, remember that Chris told us that he and Hal and Miles shared a pizza Thursday night?"

Zack nodded. "So?"

"And they were the only ones working late, right?"

Zack nodded. "So?"

"So," Kelly said, leaning forward on her knees, *"why was a Chinese food delivery guy here?"*

▲   ▼   ▲

Slater smashed a return to Marcee. Marcee had asked for a rematch after their game on Saturday. Slater had been so unsettled by Jessie's indifference on Saturday that he'd put all his energy into tennis and beat Marcee to a pulp. It turned out that Marcee was a sore loser. When it came to sports, she had a killer instinct.

Marcee smashed a shot back to the corner of the court. Slater had to run to return it. She was a much better tennis player than Jessie was. She wore her skirts shorter, too. Of course, her legs weren't as great as Jessie's, but . . .

Suddenly, Slater stopped right in the middle of the court. Marcee's shot hit him right in the chest. Right where his heart would be. If he could ever find the sucker. Jessie was right. He hadn't a clue.

It had just hit him, just like that. *Why was he always comparing Marcee with Jessie?*

"Whoa, what a space case," Marcee called. "I am sure. Like, you just stood there. My serve."

Slater tossed the ball back automatically. Every single cell in his body was screaming *oh, no!*

He couldn't still be in love with Jessie. He had fought so hard *not* to keep loving that maddening, frustrating, adorable ball of confusion. And he'd won!

He *had*, Slater told himself as Marcee's serve zoomed by him.

"Hel-*lo*!" Marcee called merrily. "Are we awake over there, hot stuff?"

Hadn't he?

Because if he hadn't, he might have a problem on his hands. Jessie was definitely not interested in him any longer. She'd let him cancel their study sessions. She'd told him she thought Great Bear was probably academically underrated. And she'd even told him that she thought Marcee was cute! She had smiled so hard at Marcee yesterday, Slater was afraid her face might crack. Jessie couldn't be that good of an actress.

"A.C.!" Marcee's voice rose a notch. "Come on!"

Could she?

Slater walked toward the net. "Marcee?" he called. "Can we talk?"

▲   ▼   ▲

"Look at this," Lisa said. "The delivery guy was here for twenty minutes. What was he doing?"

"Is he the spy, or did he come to meet the spy?" Kelly wondered, her eyes on the computer monitor.

"I don't know," Zack said. "But we're getting closer. That was really smart of you, Kelly. You get the Detective of the Year award."

"I hate to bring it up," Screech said, "but we still haven't ordered any food."

"You know what I've always wondered?" Lisa said, stretching out on the carpet. "I had this talk with your dad about his product integrity department, Zack. He said it was one of the crucial departments in the company, so he hired the best. He said he thought they were the finest team assembled in southern California. How could they have missed these bugs?"

"I've been thinking about that, too, Lisa," Screech said. "Sure, the bugs were really hidden.

But I took a look at the tests the product integrity department was running, and it was almost like the spy knew exactly what areas to avoid when planting the bugs. Almost like he knew what was going on."

"Maybe the spy is *in* the product integrity department," Kelly said.

"Maybe," Zack said. "Or maybe he has access to the tests they're running. The only people who do are Dad and Miles Moriarity."

"Funny how his name keeps coming up," Kelly said. "Not your dad, Zack. Miles."

"Not to change the subject, but are we going to order any food?" Screech said. "I'm starving."

"Excuse me?" A pretty young woman with her black hair pulled back in a ponytail poked her head in the door. "I'm looking for Eunice. Mrs. Smedley. Have you seen her?"

"I don't think she's here today," Zack said.

"You must be Zack," the woman said, smiling. "I'm Bernice Moody. I have to thank you for that pizza you sent over the other day. It was delicious."

Zack looked blank. "Pizza?"

"Eunice brought it over. She said you couldn't finish it."

"Oh, right," Zack said. "No problem."

"Eunice is so thoughtful," the woman said. "I don't know what I would have done without her.

I was all nervous and everything, being in a new job. I could always talk to her and share my problems."

"Yeah, she's a sweet lady," Zack agreed.

Bernice started to leave, and Zack suddenly shot to his feet. "Uh, Ms. Moody?"

She poked her head back in. "Yes?"

"What department do you work for?"

"The product integrity department," she said pleasantly. "Why?"

"No reason," Zack croaked. "Thanks."

Bernice left. They heard her footsteps going down the hall.

"Zack," Kelly whispered. "You can't suspect Mrs. Smedley."

"I don't know what to think," Zack said. "All I know is that she's the one who has keys to all the outer doors. She could have been here last Thursday night and nobody would have known. And she happens to have befriended someone in the product integrity department. Who knows what information Bernice has passed along without realizing it?"

"I don't believe it," Lisa said. "Not that sweet older woman."

"Why don't we access her employee records, Screech," Zack said. "It can't hurt."

Screech got to work on the computer. Within

seconds, Mrs. Smedley's background was scrolling down the screen.

"This isn't helping, Zack," Kelly said. "I mean, it's nice that we know that Eunice Smedley was born in Portland, Oregon, and that she can type over a hundred words a minute, but how can we tell if she's a spy?"

"Look at all the companies she's worked for," Lisa said. "She's super experienced. Why would she jeopardize her job?"

"Wait a sec," Screech said. He pointed to the list of companies where Mrs. Smedley had worked. "Technopro is out of business. So is QualityBrands."

"Didn't SpectroSystems put out that defective software?" Lisa asked. "I remember my mom bought it for our computer and we sent it back. We got a refund and everything."

"You're right, Lisa," Screech said excitedly. "Technopro had the same problem. It sent out software that went haywire. I read about it in *UserFriendly* magazine. That's why the company went out of business."

"That's so weird," Kelly said. "Do you think Mrs. Smedley is some kind of jinx?"

"It seems like a wild coincidence that she worked at all these companies that went out of business," Lisa agreed.

"Unless she gave them all a push," Zack said.

Suddenly, Screech's computer began beeping.

"What's that?" Kelly asked.

"I programmed the computer to tell me when the Chinese food guy signed in downstairs and was entered into the system," Screech said. "He's in the building right now!"

Chapter 12

▼ ▲ ▼ ▲ ▼

Everybody jumped up at once and ran toward the door. They collided in the doorway.

"Wait a second," Zack said. "Where are we going?"

"Follow me," Screech said. "I've got a hunch."

Screech led the way, racing down the hall toward the stairway. They followed him upstairs to the third floor, where he put a finger to his lips. Slowly, the gang tiptoed down the hall until Screech stopped in front of an office door. He pointed.

Zack put his ear to the door. He heard the clack of computer keys.

"Almost done," someone said.

He opened the door. Mrs. Smedley was sitting

on the windowsill, lifting chopsticks full of noodles to her mouth. A computer was set on a filing cabinet in the empty office, and the delivery boy was typing away.

"Stop!" Zack ordered.

"What's the matter, Zack?" Mrs. Smedley said, jumping up and knocking over the Chinese food carton. "Is something wrong?"

"Why is the Chinese food delivery guy working on our computer?" Zack asked.

"He's checking on my order," Mrs. Smedley said glibly. "I definitely ordered pork fried rice, and this is shrimp lo mein."

"Come off it, sister," Screech snarled. "We're on to you."

Mrs. Smedley gave a glacial smile. "I beg your pardon?"

"We figured it out, Mrs. Smedley," Zack said. "We followed the trail, and the trail led right to you. *You're* the industrial spy."

"Don't bother to deny it," Kelly said.

The delivery guy got up. "I think I'd better get back to work."

Zack stepped in front of him. "You're not going anywhere."

Screech moved over to the computer and cleared the screen. "That's right."

"What do you think you can do to us?" Mrs.

Smedley said, leaning back against the windowsill. "You don't have any proof."

"We know all about you," Screech said. "We know that you've gone from software company to software company and sabotaged their products."

Mrs. Smedley gave a lazy shrug. "So you say."

"We're going to prosecute," Zack warned. "My father has everything tied up in this business."

"Try scaring someone your own size, kid," Mrs. Smedley said, suddenly fierce. "I've got Infotech lawyers backing me up. We'll tie you up in court for years."

"Infotech?" Screech squeaked. "They're behind this?" He lowered his voice. "I mean, they're behind this. We knew that."

"They know how to do business," Mrs. Smedley said. "If competing software is coming out, they either buy up the company or destroy it. Thanks to us."

The delivery guy shifted from foot to foot. "I don't think you should say any more, Mom."

"Be quiet, Freddy," Mrs. Smedley said. "They're just kids. They can't do anything to me."

"How could you do this?" Kelly asked. "Mr. Morris worked so hard to get this company off the ground. He sank every dime into it."

Mrs. Smedley turned on her furiously. "Why should he make money off his software? I never did!"

"What are you talking about?" Lisa asked. "You're Mr. Morris's secretary. Why should *you* make money off his software?"

"She's not talking about *this* software," Screech said. "She's talking about Ernest Zeiderbaum's software."

"Wait," Lisa said. "I'm confused."

"She's Ernest Zeiderbaum's ex-wife," Screech said. "And I guess Freddy here is his son, right?"

Mrs. Smedley nodded, her face tight. "And he inherited his father's brilliance. At least he didn't inherit his father's stupidity along with it. Freddy knows that money is the most important thing. I raised him right."

"I don't think so," Lisa murmured.

"Oh, that's easy for you to say," Mrs. Smedley said, turning on Lisa. "Easy when you're not married to a man who designs brilliant programs but refuses to charge for them! People were making *millions* off his ideas and we were living in a one-room apartment and driving a twenty-year-old car! Do you know what the future is, children? The future is *information.* Who controls it and who can access it will determine who has power. And Ernest believed that all information should be *free!* He was a madman. I took back my maiden name and left with baby Freddy. And now I have a glamorous life. Freddy and I take six months off every year. We travel. We stay in the best hotels. No more one-room apartments for me!"

"Nice speech," Zack said. "You can tell it to the judge."

Mrs. Smedley snorted. "Dream on, as you kids say."

"Yeah," Freddy said. "Dream on."

"Without proof, what can you do?" she said. She pointed to Screech. "I'll just say that he messed up the system, working on the computer all week. The amateur. What did you call him, Zack? The jinx."

"*We* don't have to tell anybody anything," Zack said. "Because you just spilled all the beans, Mrs. Smedley."

Mrs. Smedley looked nervous. "What are you talking about, you worms?"

"Cruncher and I hooked up microphones on all the computers in the company," Screech said. "When I cleared the screen, I activated this one. By now, Chris has alerted Miles and Hal, who are listening, too. Not only did they hear this conversation, but it's being recorded."

"And Miles has probably already called the police," Zack said.

Mrs. Smedley's face was purple. "You can't do this!"

"We just did," Zack said.

The whine of a police siren began to grow louder. Mrs. Smedley paled. Freddy looked scared.

"Don't worry, Freddy," Mrs. Smedley said. She picked up the phone. "I'll call my lawyer."

But when Mrs. Smedley reached Infotech, she kept getting put on hold, even when she screamed at the person on the end of the line that she was about to get arrested. Freddy nervously ate the rest of the shrimp lo mein.

"Stop eating!" she snapped.

"It's probably my last decent meal," Freddy whined.

The police burst into the office, and Mrs. Smedley slammed down the phone. Within minutes, the police had handcuffed the pair and taken them away. Zack, Kelly, Lisa, and Screech watched them from the window as they were driven away in the police car.

"So tell me, Screech," Lisa said. "How did you know which office Mrs. Smedley was in?"

"And how did you know she'd been married to Ernest Zeiderbaum?" Kelly asked.

"Well, she was born in Portland," Screech said. "That was a good clue. That's Ernest's home town, too. But mostly I figured it out because I noticed a pattern."

"What kind of pattern?" Lisa asked.

"Well, gosh, it seemed weird to me, the way the

spy jumped from terminal to terminal. It seemed random, and hackers are never random. On the computer, each terminal has a letter code. There are twenty-seven terminals in the company, which leaves one left over. That's Zack's dad. His terminal code is *A-1*. Hal's is the letter *E*. Miles's is *Z*. I wrote all the letters down in my notes when the spy sneaked on to the system. I started to notice that the letters made sense."

Screech took out his notebook. Written on a clean page was

E Z M O N E

"Easy money," Kelly said.

"Ernest Zeiderbaum's nickname was E.Z.," Screech continued. "That was the name of his company, E.Z. Software Systems. That's when I put Mrs. Smedley and Ernest together. And that's how I knew the spy would be working on terminal *Y*, which was this office. Simple, yes?"

Lisa, Kelly, and Zack exchanged glances.

"Simple, no," Lisa said.

"I lost him after 'Well, gosh,'" Kelly said.

Zack clapped Screech on the shoulder. "I never thought I'd say this," he said, "but I respect your logic, Screech."

▲   ▼   ▲

"So," Jessie said to Slater, "what would you like to start with today?" They were sitting in the Spano rec room, and Slater was channel surfing. He bounced from a golf match to an old movie to a shopping network.

"Maybe you should turn off the TV," Jessie added pointedly.

"Whoa, cool," Slater said. "I always wanted an expandable fishing pole."

"The makeup test is tomorrow," Jessie said.

"I can study with the TV on," Slater said.

"Oh," Jessie said. "Sure."

Slater gave an exaggerated yawn. "Gosh, I'm tired."

"Up late last night?" Jessie asked.

"Date with Marcee," Slater replied.

"Oh," Jessie said. She opened her notebook.

"Then we played tennis today."

"That's nice."

She looked completely unconcerned, Slater thought worriedly. The truth was that he had been up late studying. Ever since he'd talked to the team, he'd spent every moment he could at his books. He had the material down cold at last. But he didn't want Jessie to know that.

Jessie flipped a page over. "Did you have a good time last night?" she asked in a polite tone.

"Good? I had a *fantastic* time," Slater said. "We didn't do much, though. Just went to the beach. Just me, Marcee, and a blanket. You can imagine the possibilities."

"I'd rather not," Jessie muttered. "I just ate."

"What was that?" Slater asked hopefully.

"I said, it sounds like fun," Jessie said.

"Marcee is incredible," he said. "I think older women are the best."

"She's only a year older than you, Slater," Jessie said.

"That one year makes a big difference," Slater said. "I don't know what it is. Maybe it's college. It matures a person, I guess. Because Marcee is so . . . sophisticated and interesting."

Jessie swallowed. "Mmmmm."

"And so *smart*, too," Slater added.

"Wow," Jessie murmured. "Really."

"What was that?"

"I said, I can tell," Jessie said.

"Sophisticated, but somehow simple, too—"

"Now, that's obvious," Jessie said.

"What?"

"I was just agreeing with you," Jessie said sweetly.

"Maybe we could double-date sometime," Slater offered, watching Jessie carefully. Was her face starting to get just a little pink? She just had to still care for him!

"That would be great," Jessie said enthusiastically.

"Of course, I'd have to clear it with Marcee," Slater went on. "She doesn't like to share me. But I just know the two of you would get along. I wonder where we could go . . . someplace Marcee would feel comfortable—"

"How about the playground?" Jessie snarled.

"What?"

Jessie slammed the book shut. "I said, how about the playground? Marcee would fit right in. *Really*. But, like, I don't know if she could follow the conversations in the sandbox. They might be over her head!"

Slater felt joy shoot through him. He put a hand to his heart. "I'm shocked. Shocked that you would talk about Marcee this way!"

"And you think we'd *like* each other?" Jessie said hotly. "You think I'd have one tiny thing in common with that addle-brained, simpering, bouncing piece of bubble gum? She can't even, like, speak English. I'd have to go to the mall to find an interpreter!"

Slater began to chortle. "Sounds to me like you're jealous."

"Jealous! Ha! Of that shrimp?"

"Jealous because you're still crazy about me," Slater said, crossing his arms.

"Hold on, Mr. Ego," Jessie returned. "It has nothing to do with you. I just don't like to see you set your sights so low, Slater. It's the same reason I wasn't crazy about you going to Great Bear. You can do better. You're a lot smarter, and you have so much on the ball. You could be anything you wanted to be, Slater."

Suddenly, Jessie realized that she was about to cry. "Not that it matters to me. Because it doesn't. Because it's your life, and . . . and I'm not part of it anymore, and—"

"I wish you were," Slater said.

"—and," Jessie continued, "I've accepted that you're going to move on, so I—what did you say?"

"I wish you were still part of my life," Slater said simply.

Jessie's mouth hung open in surprise. "You do?"

He leaned over and gently closed her mouth. Then he kissed it. "Call me crazy, but I do," he murmured.

"You're crazy," Jessie said breathlessly. "But I'm crazy, too."

Slater leaned over and kissed her again. He couldn't imagine why he'd ever thought he'd be able to stop wanting to kiss Jessie Spano. The girl was in his blood, for better or for worse.

The phone rang, and they broke apart. Jessie sighed. "I'd better answer it. It might be my mom."

She picked it up and said hello. Slater leaned back, listening, as she said "Yes," and "Uh-huh," and "Of course." She ended the conversation with "He's right here. Okay, we'll be right there."

"Where will we be?" Slater said. He slipped his arms around her again. "I was just getting started."

"I know," Jessie said. She bit her lip worriedly. "But it's Zack. He needs us."

"On a Sunday night?" Slater said. "Why? Can't he program his VCR?"

"He said he'd explain when we got there," Jessie said. "But he needs help moving some furniture."

Chapter 13

▼ ▲ ▼ ▲ ▼

Zack was sitting down to a home-cooked meal for the first time in what seemed like ages. His mother came toward the dining room table, carrying a platter high in the air. Steam rose as a tempting aroma filled his nostrils. Zack was so sick of pizza and Chinese food and cheeseburgers. He couldn't wait to see what his mother had prepared.

"Close your eyes, Zack," she urged, smiling. Slowly, he closed them. "Let me give you a taste."

Feeling like a kid of seven again, Zack opened his mouth. He waited for something delicious to slide across his tongue. Instead, it was fibrous and scratchy, with a little grit mixed in. Zack opened his eyes and discovered that on his plate was a huge slab of . . . carpet!

Zack awoke with a start. His cheek was pressed against the carpet in his father's office. His mouth was slightly open, and he tasted polyester. He spat out a tiny thread on his tongue.

He sat up slowly, rubbing his cheek where the woolly pattern of the rug had left red welts. He felt stiff and exhausted, but he didn't care. The job was done.

Screech was asleep across the room on Mr. Morris's desk, his head pillowed in his arms. He had worked all night with Miles, Chris, and Hal to get every single bug out of Timesaver.

Meanwhile, Zack, Kelly, Lisa, Slater, and Jessie had moved all the furniture back into the offices. Acme had agreed to deliver their low-priced line on a Sunday but had refused to install it. The gang had ridden up and down on the freight elevators all night and had pulled dollies and pushed furniture back into offices.

Zack smiled, remembering how Jessie had passed the time by quizzing Slater on the Bill of Rights. Slater would be pushing a dolly loaded with filing cabinets down the hall and Jessie would yell, *"What was the Nineteenth Amendment?"*

It had been a wild, busy night, and it was over. Zack had sent the girls home around two A.M., when their parents had called for the tenth time. Mrs. Spano, Mrs. Kapowski, and the Turtles had been okay about letting the girls stay out late, but enough was enough. Slater hadn't left until the last bookcase had been filled and the last lamp had been plugged back in.

Zack went over and gently nudged Screech.

"Mom?" Screech said.

"It's me, Screech."

"Dad?"

"It's Zack."

Screech opened his eyes. "Zack? What are you doing in my bedroom?"

Zack grinned. "Come on, cowboy. Time to herd 'em up and move 'em out. School starts in an hour."

Screech yawned and slid off the desk. "When does your dad get here?"

Zack looked at his watch. "Any minute. I'm going to hang out and wait for him. I'll see you at school."

Screech left, and Zack wandered out to see if he could start the coffee in the employees' lunchroom. When he came back with a steaming cup, his father had already arrived.

"Dad! You're here," Zack said. "Boy, do I have a lot to tell you."

His father grinned. "Miles already filled me in. I stopped at his office. I'm really proud of you, son. You handled everything like a pro. And you saved my company."

Zack shrugged. "I had plenty of help."

His father put an arm around Zack's shoulders.

"It takes a leader to organize that kind of effort. And unmasking Mrs. Smedley was brilliant."

Zack squirmed uncomfortably. There was nothing he'd like better than to bask in the glow. It wasn't often that his father congratulated him on an achievement. Usually, he was looking over his glasses at him and saying "How could this have happened, Zack?" Or: "When are you going to live up to your potential, son?" Or even: "Don't tell me. Not again."

He'd love to take all the credit, but he couldn't. "It was Screech, Dad," he said. "He's the one who really figured out what was going on."

Mr. Morris nodded. "Screech did some incredible work. No question about it. In fact, Miles just had a suggestion. He wants to hire Screech part-time. He was really impressed. So am I."

"Wow, that's great," Zack said. "Screech will flip." And nobody would ever call his pal a jinx again, Zack vowed. He knew *he* never would.

"But I'm really impressed with you, Zack," Mr. Morris said. "Thank you for my company. Thank you for working so hard to save it."

"I know how much it means to you, Dad," Zack said. He gave his father a hug.

"There's only one tiny problem," Mr. Morris said with a frown.

"Uh-oh," Zack said. "Did you find another bug?"

Mr. Morris surveyed the office and focused on the brown tweed sofa. "What happened to my leather couch?"

▲   ▼   ▲

Later that afternoon, Slater burst into the lunchroom and sauntered to the gang's usual table. He waved a white paper in the air.

"Don't tell me," Jessie said. "I can tell by your face. You passed."

Slater waggled the paper in her face. "Not only did I *pass*, momma. I got an *A*."

"Oh, my gosh!" Jessie squealed. She jumped up and threw her arms around Slater. "I'm so proud of you!"

She kissed Slater, and the gang exchanged glances.

"Hey, hold on," Lisa said. "That was definitely not a *friendly* kiss. That was a *girlfriend* kiss."

"What's going on?" Kelly asked the two suspiciously.

"Don't tell me you're back together," Lisa said.

"Well . . . ," Slater said uneasily.

"Um, actually . . . ," Jessie said.

"Zack, can you believe this?" Kelly asked. "Zack?"

She looked over. Zack had fallen asleep on a pile of books. "Poor guy," she said softly. She put her finger to her lips to warn the gang.

"It's going to be different this time," Slater whispered. "Honest."

Lisa rolled her eyes. "Yeah, right," she said in a low tone so that she wouldn't wake up Zack. "My momma didn't raise a dummy, Slater. You say that every time."

"This time is different," Jessie insisted in a whisper.

"Yeah," Slater said. "We're both going to see other people at the same time."

"*What?*" Kelly, Lisa, and Screech bellowed.

Zack woke up with a start. "Mom, don't make me eat that carpet! Wha—what's happening?"

"Slater and Jessie are back together," Kelly said.

Zack dropped his head back on his books with a groan. "Then I'm definitely going back to sleep. Wake me when they break up again."

"You don't understand," Slater said. "Jessie and I are two different people now. We're open to new people, new experiences."

"Yeah, look at Slater," Jessie said. "He just got an *A* on a test. If that isn't a new experience, I don't know what is."

Slater grinned. "You see what I mean? Besides, Jessie didn't mind when I was dating Marcee. She took it like a pro. I mean, I'm not saying it won't *bother* us to see each other with other people. But we're grown-ups. We can take it."

Jessie's smile got a little strained. "Right."

"You should have seen how cool and collected Jessie was," Slater told the gang. "I had to really push her to get her to react. Otherwise, she would have been fine."

Jessie nodded stiffly. "I was fine," she said in a too-bright voice.

But Slater didn't notice. "For instance, we're not seeing each other Friday night."

"We're each going to do our own thing," Jessie said.

"I'm taking Marcee to the movies," Slater said.

Kelly and Lisa watched, fascinated, as Jessie's face got red, then deepened into purple.

"And Jessie doesn't mind a bit," Slater said.

"Really, Jessie?" Kelly asked.

Jessie gulped. "Really," she said.

Don't miss the next HOT novel about the "SAVED BY THE BELL" gang

SILVER SPURS

Zack and the gang head out to a dude ranch for some fun and excitement. When they get there, Zack is mistaken for a real-life rodeo star!

But can he learn to throw a lasso before all the cowgirls discover he's not the genuine article? Find out in the next "Saved by the Bell" novel.